ISLE OF INTRIGUE

Selina has come to Tarango to take up her inheritance — her father's sugar plantation — and she falls in love with the place from the moment of her arrival. There she meets the strikingly handsome Zack Halliday, who wants to buy her out, as does Hank Wayne, a tough American who won't take no for an answer. Then Fiona Stuart appears, wilful and jealous. Selina suspects the worst — and subsequent events prove her right . . .

PHYLLIS MALLETT

ISLE OF INTRIGUE

Complete and Unabridged

LINFORD
Leicester

First published in Great Britain in 1997

First Linford Edition
published 2013

A catalogue record for this book is available
from the British Library.

ISBN 978–1–4448–1647–1

Published by
F. A. Thorpe (Publishing)
Anstey, Leicestershire

Set by Words & Graphics Ltd.
Anstey, Leicestershire
Printed and bound in Great Britain by
T. J. International Ltd., Padstow, Cornwall

This book is printed on acid-free paper

1

Selina was eager to get her first glimpse of Tarango, an island set like a polished jewel in the glittering blue waters of the Caribbean. Her green eyes shone as she narrowed them against the glare of the sun to peer through the porthole of the seaplane carrying her on the last lap of the journey from London.

A gasp escaped her when she spotted a line of white foam where huge waves were thundering on a coral reef, and for a frightening moment it seemed that the small aircraft would splash down into the very centre of the tumult. But the reef dropped behind and the plane skimmed the smooth surface of the bay beyond, speeding towards its anchorage.

She sighed. At last she had arrived! But the sad thing was that Father was not here to greet her. Her parents had parted twenty years before, Mother taking Selina to England and never telling her about Tarango, the place she was born.

She had learned nothing about her father until Mother, in her last few days, revealed the facts surrounding her origins. Even then she had to wait until after Mother's funeral before the full truth was revealed, and she discovered that her father had died three years earlier and Selina had inherited his sugar cane plantation on Tarango.

The seaplane bobbed on the swell in the bay, which was surrounded by tall cliffs. Suddenly, Selina was gripped by an irrational panic as she realised, for the first time since the news broke, that she was on the brink of the unknown.

The sun was glaring in a brazen, copper-coloured sky, and she sighed at the memory of the dreary life she had left behind in London. She knew she was taking a gamble starting afresh but on the island, it seemed the only thing to do after the painful end of a relationship at home.

A crowd was standing on the stone quay, and Selina could feel a touch of unreality as the cheerful pilot helped her ashore and set down her luggage. A throng of colourful natives pressed around her, and she was surrounded by men asking if they could carry her baggage. But she was being met by someone from the plantation, so she waited patiently as the crowd dispersed. Finally, she was alone. She looked around, exhausted, despite her excitement.

The heat of the sun clung to her, almost sizzling on the quay. She was wearing light trousers and a white blouse that now felt damp and clinging. Her long blonde hair was tied up for the journey, and she could feel perspiration gathering on her brow.

What she wouldn't give for a cold shower, she thought, wondering what had happened to the man appointed to pick her up. Paul Clarke, who had managed Father's plantation for thirty years, was supposed to have been waiting for her!

A car suddenly appeared from along the street and pulled on to the quay a few yards from where Selina was standing. She watched as a man got out. He was about thirty years old, at least six feet tall and powerfully built.

She experienced a flutter of awareness, her gaze held by the force of his eyes as they surveyed her, taking in all the details of her slender body as he smiled perfunctorily and moved towards her.

He was too young to be Paul Clarke, she thought. But he was quite handsome, with his fair, wavy hair, his tanned face and striking bone structure. But the feature Selina felt most drawn to were his icy blue eyes.

As he looked into her green eyes she got the impression there were deep undercurrents of intense emotion beneath his hard exterior, and her attention seemed to be captured against her will. She didn't usually pay so much attention to strangers but he was worthy of a second look, and his jutting chin, with its faint suspicion of a cleft, warned that there was a ruthlessness not to be toyed with.

'Selina Carr?' His voice was deep and rich.

'Yes! Are you from the plantation?' she replied somewhat hesitantly.

'Not yours!'

He smiled, and Selina felt an alarming shiver travel down her spine. She wasn't used to reacting involuntarily to men in this way.

'I'm Zack Halliday, your neighbour. Paul Clarke, your manager, is stranded, broken down, at the roadside, and when I passed him he asked me to pick you up.'

His gaze flickered again over her slender body from head to toe, noting every detail. Her red-gold hair framed the soft shape of her face, eyes narrowed against the sunlight, and as she moistened her lips, she sighed heavily, realising that she must present a dishevelled picture, travel-stained and exhausted as she was.

'Thank you for your trouble. I hope it doesn't take you out of your way.'

'Out here we try to help anyone who needs it.'

His smile was slightly crooked, the only imperfection she noticed about him, but it only added to his attractiveness.

'In fact,' he added, a flash of some obscure emotion in his pale eyes, 'there's something I'd like to discuss with you.'

Selina's frown was derived as much from the glare of the sun as his words, but suddenly alarms were sounding in her mind. She'd never met this man in her life before and yet here he was, telling her there was something he wanted to discuss.

'I'll tell you about it on the drive to your place.'

He took hold of her arm and turned to escort her to his car.

'My luggage!' she gasped.

The warmth of his hand on her bare

flesh sent shivers darting through her, and there was a tingle in her arm at their point of contact.

He signalled to a nearby native who immediately rushed over, picked up the luggage and stowed it safely in the boot of Zack's car. He was obviously well-known around these parts.

'Are you taking me straight to the plantation?' Selina asked.

She drew a deep breath as he slid into the car and started the engine.

'Yes. And I'm glad to be the first to get to you. You can expect to be chased around the island as soon as news of your arrival gets out.'

'I don't understand.' She was starting to get a bit weary of his habit of talking in riddles. 'Perhaps you would explain.'

Instead of answering, he concentrated on driving, taking the car off the quay and into a street crowded with vehicles, some very old and decrepit.

'There's been some speculation here about your intentions,' Zack replied eventually. 'Rumours have been flying since we found out that Henry Carr's unknown daughter in England was finally coming over.'

'I still don't understand,' she said, shaking her head.

'It's quite simple. A number of people have been awaiting your arrival with growing interest because your plantation has become a desirable property.'

'Someone wants to buy it?' Selina was amazed. 'But I have no intention of selling!'

'I had a sneaking feeling you'd say that.' He smiled as he glanced at her. 'I don't expect you'll last long out here, away from the bright lights. Six months at the most! You don't look the type to rough it in these surroundings.' His tone was more than a little cynical. 'It won't be long before you sell up and fly back to England!'

'Thank you!' Selina could not believe his attitude. 'Obviously you're one of those interested in buying the planta-tion!' She watched him as he continued to stare ahead. 'And if that's the case then why should I consider selling to you? If there is more than one interested buyer and I planned to sell, then the sensible thing to do would be to go to auction!'

'That would depend on how you feel about the plantation. I was assuming you would naturally hold your father's convictions.'

'I never knew my father so I never came under his influence! I was taken from the island before I was old enough to know anyone.'

'Your father has been dead three years and you've just arrived!'

There was flat accusation in his voice, and Selina flinched at the hostility in his eyes as he glanced at her. She was shocked by it, her determination filtering away as she gazed ahead.

'So your attitude is an unknown quantity,' he went on. 'And my best advice to you is take a few days to acclimatise, and when you are rested perhaps we could get together for a business discussion.'

'I've already said I have no intention of selling the plantation!'

'That's fine as far as it goes. But in this world everything is for sale. It's all a matter of getting the right price. All I would ask at this stage is that you don't give a certain Hank Wayne an option to buy until we have had an opportunity to talk.'

'Hank Wayne?'

Selina shook her head, wondering what on earth had been developing here on the island in her absence.

'Who is Hank Wayne?' she asked outright.

'An American property developer who wants to turn Tarango into a holiday playground and ruin it for everyone who lives here.'

His tone had hardened imperceptibly and his chin jutted aggressively.

'Ah!' She nodded. 'Now I'm beginning to see a light! And what would you do with the plantation if you managed to buy it?'

'Keep it as a plantation and preserve its natural beauty.'

She didn't reply; and when he remained silent, she turned her attention to the exotic surroundings. From time to time she had caught glimpses of blue sea beyond the cliffs on the right as the car followed the coast road but his voice had been distracting her. Now she was able to study the rather inhospitable cliffs. She was aware that Tarango had originally been formed by volcanic action, and when she looked inland, she saw the volcano itself, rearing its stark height to dominate the entire island.

To her left were hosts of colourful flowers and lush green vegetation, while dark trees covered the rising ground surrounding the lower slopes of the volcano. The heat was terrific, and she was glad to be wearing her lightest clothes.

A sugar cane truck suddenly appeared, coming towards them at a fantastic speed, leaving a cloud of dust in its wake. Zack muttered as he pulled over to the side of the road to give the vehicle plenty of room, as it went dashing by, horn blaring.

'If you ever meet one of those fellows when you're driving then give him a wide berth,' he said. 'They have no road sense and seem intent on destroying themselves and everyone they encounter.'

Selina relaxed her shoulders. Her head was now aching from the continual glare of the brilliant sunlight.

'Is it far to my place?' she enquired.

'Another two miles or so.'

'And where is your plantation in relation to mine.'

'Inland. We're neighbours, although my house is ten miles from yours.'

'And is anyone trying to buy you out?'

'No!' he replied, laughing harshly. 'You own the only frontage on Barracuda Bay, which has the only beach on the island, an essential commodity for tourists. The beach is what makes your

12

estate so desirable.'

'I see! That's very interesting!'

He was silent as they rounded a sharp bend overlooking the cliffs, and Selina's attention was caught by a breathtaking view of Barracuda Bay. Just below lay a fringe of yellow sand between sea and cliffs that stretched around the gentle curve of the bay for as far as she could see. She became aware of a roaring sound and looked across the bay to see, far out, huge waves crashing on a coral reef that protected the bay from the open sea.

Her gaze followed the line of cliffs around the bay and she caught her breath when her narrowed eyes alighted on a two-storey house standing on a cliff overlooking the cove.

'Is that my house?' she asked, emotion constricting her throat as she sensed she was looking at the place where she had been born.

'It is. You seem quite impressed!'

'I've never seen anything so beautiful!'

Her eyes sparkled, and for a moment the painful memory of what lay behind in England filled her mind, trying to spoil the pleasure of this moment. But she quashed it, determined not to let anything mar the new beginning she had planned.

'Most visitors are of the same opinion when they see this for the first time! Then they become accustomed to the island and don't even notice the beauty any more,' he added rather moodily.

She ignored this challenge, her gaze drinking in the scene before her.

'Paul Clarke, your estate manager, and his wife have been living in your house since your father died,' he continued. 'They have a smaller place farther along the cliffs which you can't see from here.'

Selina tried to relax as he drove on. She had not been prepared for this exotic view, or the apparent situation awaiting her, and wondered what other surprises might be in store.

As they drew nearer the house, she saw a grey roof and very tall chimneys. The long windows were like gaping eyes in the bright sunlight, but brightly-coloured curtains softened their stark appearance. The walls had been painted a pale pink and the white woodwork gleamed in the sun. There was a wide veranda at ground level, which gave adequate shade, and tall trees sur-rounded the building.

Thoughts of her father surfaced in Selina's mind. If only he had lived longer! She couldn't even remember what he looked like, and her mother had not once mentioned him after leaving the island.

During Selina's formative years, when she had often asked about her father, Mother had given no details beyond stating that he had died many years before. So Mother's death-bed revelation had been a great shock, and Selina was deeply upset that she had not been given the opportunity to meet and get to know her father.

Sudden tears stung her eyes and she blinked rapidly. This was not the time for sadness! She had impressed that fact on herself before leaving London. This was to be the start of a new life.

She saw Zack watching her. He looked so cool, and there was a sense of belonging about him which indicated that he was native to the island. She, however, was rootless although she had been born here. But she had been uprooted almost before she had been able to walk. A sigh escaped her as she reaffirmed her vow that it would not be long before she slipped into this new way of life.

The car turned in at a wide gateway and Zack drove along a rutted track that led to the house. There was no formal garden, but great clumps of exotic flowers were growing in profusion, and she was uplifted by the knowledge that she was here to stay in this tropical paradise where she had been born. They halted beside a flight of stone steps that led to a veranda and a wire screen door, and as Selina alighted from the car, a middle-aged woman emerged from the house, pausing on the veranda.

'Hello,' she greeted quietly. 'I'm Joanne, Paul's wife. I'm sorry Paul was unable to meet you on the quay. He telephoned about his car, which had to be towed to a garage. But luckily Zack was available!'

'I'm glad to have been of service,' Zack cut in. 'It enabled me to have a chat with Selina!'

He smiled when Selina glanced at him.

'I was on my way to an important meeting at the bank when I saw Paul at the roadside. I can now safely leave you in Joanne's capable hands, Selina, but I'll return shortly.'

He turned to depart, and Selina called after him as he was getting into his car.

'My luggage is in your boot!'

He grimaced and shrugged, then turned to open the boot of the car.

'Selina, you must be very tired after your trip, and it didn't help that no-one was at the quay to greet you,' Joanne was saying.

Joanne was tall and slender, probably in her middle fifties. She had a homely face that was lined around the eyes by too much sun, and her hair was grey-streaked.

'Paul sounded upset when he phoned,' she added.

'Breakdowns can't be avoided!'

Selina shrugged as Zack returned with her luggage, suddenly aware that the sun beating on her head was causing great discomfort. Then, to her horror, she began to lose her sense of balance.

'Zack, come quickly,' Joanne called.

Selina tried to fight off the encroaching darkness that hovered in her head, and dimly heard her luggage drop to the ground as hurried footsteps came towards her. The next instant she was seized by a pair of powerful arms and lifted bodily, being held so tightly that she was almost stifled. Her sight and hearing faded and she was only dimly aware of Zack speaking to Joanne.

'It must be the heat. Lead the way and I'll carry her in,' he said.

Selina fell against his chest with her head on his left shoulder. She could hear his breathing and felt the powerful beating of his heart, while the exotic tang of his aftershave did nothing to settle her senses.

'Did you get the chance to sound her out?' Joanne asked urgently as they entered the house, escaping the torture of the blazing sun, and obviously thinking that Selina wasn't aware of what was happening to her.

'Not completely! Her initial attitude is that she won't sell, but she's suffering from jet lag and the heat. I have to go into town now but I'll be back to work on her as soon as possible. Try to find out what you can while I'm away, and, whatever you do, keep Hank Wayne away from her.'

He put Selina down on a settee.

'Give her plenty of cool drinks, keep her quiet, and she'll come round,' he advised, almost like a doctor. 'I'll get her luggage.'

He turned away, leaving Selina struggling to sit up, her mind reeling in shock at his words. What was going on here? He was obviously determined to buy the plantation, and Joanne seemed to be on his side! And Hank Wayne had to be kept away from her!

Selina sighed and let her head rest against the back of the settee, keeping her eyes closed until Zack returned with her luggage, deposited it and then departed, the sound of his receding footsteps filling her with relief. Joanne came and sat at Selina's side as Selina's eyes opened.

'Have a sip of this cool juice. It will do you good,' Joanne said, sounding genuinely concerned.

Selina opened her eyes and struggled to regain her balance.

'Thank you,' she responded. 'I'll be

all right now I'm out of the sun.'

'But Zack is right. You must take things easy for a few days. It's a long trip from England, and the island will take some getting used to. When you're able, come and see the room I've prepared for you. Then you can shower and change. I'll have coffee waiting when you come down.'

'That sounds like a good idea, and I'll certainly take things easy for a few days,' Selina said with a smile.

'Leave your luggage where it is and Paul will bring it up to your room when he returns. We've been living here since your father died, to keep an eye on things, but now you've arrived, we shall have to think about moving back to our own house.'

Selina got to her feet and accompanied Joanne across a wide hall to the stairs. Out of the direct rays of the sun, she was feeling better, and began to look around with interest. There was a portrait of a middle-aged man on a wall and she caught her breath as she paused to study it, emotion constricting her throat.

'Is this my father?' she asked.

'Yes!' Joanne's voice was edged with surprise. 'Don't you know him by sight? He was always sending you photographs of himself and the island.'

Selina shook her head.

'Mother didn't keep any photographs. She never talked about Father either. Did you know my mother?'

Joanne nodded.

'It all happened so long ago, but I do remember your mother very well.'

She paused, apparently reluctant to talk on the subject.

'All I can say is there was a great deal of bitterness on both sides, and when you were taken away, your father missed you every day until his death.'

'I wish I'd known him,' Selina said softly.

'It's a great pity, the way it happened. I'm sure you would have liked him.'

Joanne led the way up the staircase. As they went, Selina was impressed by what she saw. The house was well furnished and spotlessly clean.

'This was your father's room,' Joanne said as she opened a door on the landing. 'I thought you might like to use it. It's been completely redecorated.'

Selina paused on the threshold and peered inside. It was a large room, spacious and airy. There was a pale green carpet on the floor and heavy brocade curtains in gold and green at the two windows. The single bed was new, with pale blue sheets and pillowcases.

A pine bedside cabinet had a clock and a lamp on it, and there was a dressing-table with triple adjustable mirrors. Fresh flowers in a large vase filled the air with their perfume.

'Do you like it?' Joanne was anxious. 'I spent a long time getting it ready when I heard you were coming.'

'It's perfect.' Selina smiled, her spirits rising. 'I like your taste, Joanne. I couldn't have done it better myself.'

'The bathroom is through here.' Joanne crossed the wide room and opened a door. 'Why not shower now? It will make you feel so much better.'

'Thank you, I will. I'll just fetch my small case. You've done a great job and I appreciate it.'

'I told Paul I had to do something!' Joanne replied. 'But you can always have it done again if you don't like it.'

'I wouldn't dream of changing a thing,' Selina said, smiling.

They returned downstairs, where Selina picked up her small case. Then she paused, looking at Joanne, who moved uneasily, as if deeply worried.

'I got the feeling when I arrived that there's some kind of trouble here on the island,' she said.

'Trouble?' Joanne frowned and shook her head. 'I don't understand.'

Selina recalled the snatch of conversation that had passed between Joanne and Zack and realised that Joanne would not admit anything, but it was certain that she agreed with Zack on a course of action, and the two of them were set against the unknown Hank Wayne. Obviously it had to do with Wayne's intention to develop the island, judging by Zack's initial conversation, but was that all there was to it?

'I felt there was more to Zack's conversation than he actually said,' she observed. 'And I detected an undercurrent of hostility in his manner when he met me on the quay.'

'I see!'

Joanne laughed but she was clearly troubled.

'Don't pay too much heed to Zack's manner. It wasn't you personally, I can assure you. He's still recovering from a broken romance and, at the moment, his view of women in general is rather jaundiced, to say the least.'

Selina nodded, but she was thoughtful as she returned to her room, and considered her impression while showering, luxuriating under the darting pencils of cool water that splashed against her burning skin. Afterwards, she pulled on a cotton dress and sandals. A sigh of relief escaped her as she sat at the dressing-table and tried to repair the ravages of her journey.

She was feeling almost normal now, but her thoughts were constantly troubled by Zack Halliday. She considered his words and attitude and was unconvinced. Was he only concerned that the character of the island would be sullied by development or was there something more sinister going on?

She looked out across the bay, and was awed by the sight of the massive rollers crashing on the reef. From her vantage point she was able to survey the entire bay, and the scenery was completely out of this world. No wonder Zack Halliday wanted to buy it!

She pictured his face. He was certainly a very handsome man, and he was coming back to work on her! She shivered, sensing that she ought to stay well away from him. She was here to start a new life, and had no intention of getting caught up in local entanglements.

When she went downstairs, Joanne was talking to her husband. Selina shook hands with Paul Clarke, a tall, bronzed man in his fifties. He was most apologetic for failing to meet her.

'Don't worry about it,' Selina responded. 'It could happen to anyone. I learned from Zack that my arrival has been eagerly awaited, so perhaps you'll fill me in on the situation.'

'I'll make some coffee while you two talk,' Joanne said, and departed quickly.

Paul pulled out a chair at the table and invited Selina to sit down.

'I hope the situation that's arisen won't spoil things for you,' he hedged. 'There has been growing speculation on the island for some time.'

'I won't permit anything to spoil my life,' she said firmly. 'I've come here to live, and I hope you'll do your job as if my father were still alive. Nothing is going to change.'

He nodded, suddenly eager.

'I'd like nothing better. It's been very unsettling for us since your father died. No-one knew what was going to happen, and because you didn't arrive immediately after your father died, it was assumed that you had no wish to visit and no interest in the plantation.'

'I can understand that, but that's in the past now. I'm here to stay, and I hope you might be able to teach me something of the business. I have no intention of sitting around twiddling my thumbs. I'll need to occupy my time.'

'What did you do in England?'

Joanne, returning with a tray, was in time to catch Selina's last remark, and asked the question.

'I was a secretary with an insurance company.'

Selina's voice hardened imperceptibly as she thought of David, who had been her immediate boss. Then she realised that Joanne and Paul were watching her intently and forced a smile.

The past was behind her now and that was where it would remain. She steeled herself to go on, her mind crystal clear for the first time since her mother's death.

'Zack mentioned someone named Hank Wayne who's interested in buying the plantation with the intention of turning it into a holiday complex. If that is true we shall have to make it quite clear from the outset that we are not on the market.'

'They'll get the message,' Paul promised, relief evident in his weathered features.

He smiled as he exchanged glances with Joanne, and Selina realised that any hostility she had sensed in Joanne earlier stemmed from the woman's concern for their future.

'Hank Wayne has been most reluctant to take no for an answer! He's been haunting the island for the last three years, trying to find out about you. I'm sure he made enquiries in England, but he couldn't track you down.'

'That's one thing I have to be thankful to Mother for,' Selina observed. 'She even kept my father's death from me!'

'But now we know our direction, we'll change all that,' Paul promised.

Selina nodded determinedly, but inside she was filled with conflicting emotions, aware that her new-found resolutions were wavering, and she realised that the change had started the moment she met Zack Halliday. She drew a deep breath, for the future promised to be far from dull.

2

When Selina retired that evening, her senses were blanketed by a blend of pleasure and excitement. Her new way of life had started with a speed that made her feel giddy, and with so many new impressions to be contained, her mind felt near to bursting. But she suffered an underlying sense of concern which could only be attributed to Zack.

He had not returned as intended, telephoning Joanne to say he was detained in town. Selina was keenly aware that she had been disappointed by his failure to return for he had made an impact on her. She sighed as she crossed to the window of her room to gaze into the darkness, wondering how many times her father had done the same thing during his lifetime.

A frown touched her soft features and wistfulness seized her as she thought of her father. Why hadn't she discovered his existence in time to have known him? The question was hurtful. And why had Mother been so bitter that she denied her the birthright of knowing her own father?

Sighing deeply, she looked up at the dusky, velvety sky strewn with countless, twinkling stars. Tiny, fleece-like clouds were lined with silver magic by the thin crescent moon riding high in the heavens. Its light on the smooth water of the bay projected a silver pathway between the shore and the horizon. The night was silent apart from the roar of crashing waves hammering the reef, but even that awesome sound seemed muted now, like a natural lullaby forming an exotic background to the tropical night.

Selina relaxed for the first time since her arrival and, sitting on the wide window ledge, enjoyed the scene before her. It seemed that a hundred years had passed since she left London. Tarango was working its magic, casting a spell upon her, making her recent past seem distant and unreal.

She arose eventually and made her way over to her bed, certain that at last she could rest. She slid between the scented sheets and closed her eyes, fearing excitement would ruin her sleep, but that was the last thing she remembered . . .

When she opened her eyes again, it was morning. Brilliant sunlight was slanting in at the window, and the dull sound of waves booming against the reef instantly recalled her memory and she slid out of the bed and crossed to the window. She had to squint against the glare of the sun, and the sea and the sky seemed to merge into one. In the middle distance, the waves hammered the reef ceaselessly, bursting into tumultuous white spray that dominated the calm blue water of Barracuda Bay.

She hurried to shower and dress, impatient to enjoy the sights. Descending the stairs, her thoughts returned to Zack. He was recovering from a broken romance, Joanne had said, which would account for his somewhat prickly manner.

'Good morning!'

Joanne emerged from the kitchen, smiling widely, her manner conveying the impression that any hostility she might have harboured at their meeting the day before was now non-existent. It was apparent that she had been affected by the uncertain situation that existed until Selina's arrival cleared the air.

'Did you sleep well, Selina?'

'Good morning, Joanne. Yes, I slept perfectly, thanks. I was utterly worn out from travelling. But I feel quite rested now.'

'Take my advice and relax for the next forty-eight hours,' Joanne advised with a smile.

'That sounds like good advice. Swimming won't be too strenuous, will it? The bay looks so inviting.'

'It's ideal, but try not to get too much sun at first. Come and eat some breakfast and then I'll get Alora to take you down to the beach. The bay is your private property so there'll be no-one to trouble you. There is one man I'm sure you'll want to avoid if possible, and that's Hank Wayne. Zack told you that Wayne is keen to build a yacht marina in the bay, with a hotel and leisure complex right here on the site of this house. Can you imagine anyone wanting to pull down this beautiful, old place?'

Selina shook her head as she sat down to breakfast. There would be no changes made to the estate, she vowed, her mind crammed with a host of new impressions, and she would soon make that abundantly clear. The promise of future challenges excited her, and she found it difficult to eat and relax.

Later, she changed into a bikini, then donned a beach cloak. Slipping her feet into white sandals, she was ready to start her relaxing. Alora was attractive, with fine features, and proved to be friendly and communicative as they set off for the beach.

They crossed a paved terrace to the clifftop, where a flight of wooden steps gave access to the golden beach. But the brilliant sunlight bouncing off the scintillating water made Selina's eyes ache, and she quickly searched her holdall for sun glasses, to cut down the glare.

'It's easier going down these steps than climbing them, I expect,' she observed as they descended, and Alora agreed.

There was a wide stretch of beach at the foot of the cliffs, and when they reached it, Selina was surprised to find palm trees growing out of the sand itself. She could hardly wait to get into the water, and quickly threw off her wrap and sandals. Then she spotted a towel lying at the foot of a nearby palm tree!

'Is someone here who shouldn't be, Alora?' she demanded.

'No, missy!' the girl replied. 'The towel belongs to Mr Halliday. He swims in the bay.'

'Doesn't he know it's private?'

Selina became aware of an uplifting feeling at the mention of Zack's name. She glanced around. A pang stabbed through her when she spotted his head in the water quite some distance out from the shore.

She ran to the water's edge to plunge in, and swam eagerly, delighted with the temperature of the water. She relaxed and floated. The sun was beating down fiercely, and she realised that her skin would very soon burn. But she was aware of the danger and had no intention of overdoing anything during these first days.

She could have stayed in the water all morning but eventually emerged, instinctively looking around for Zack. She was astounded to see his head very close to the line of the distant reef, and experienced a pang of alarm.

She turned her gaze to the shore in search of Alora. The girl was a hundred yards away, throwing stones into the water, evidently bored with this unusual chore of acting as a chaperone to her new mistress.

Selina pushed the knowledge of Zack's intrusion into the background and spread her towel on the hot sand and sat down. She applied a liberal quantity of lotion to her shoulders and limbs before stretching out. Then she closed her eyes with a contented sigh and let her body relax.

She drowsed luxuriously until a shadow fell across her. She was relieved by the disturbance because she sensed it was time to stop sunbathing. Opening her eyes, she looked up to see a figure silhouetted between herself and the sun. Blinded by the glare, she looked away quickly.

'Come and stand on the other side where I can see you, Alora,' she said.

The figure moved around her, and Selina sprang to her feet when she saw that it was a man. Grabbing her beach wrap, she threw it on, then looked at the stranger, who was short and thickset, about forty years old, she judged.

'Say, I'm sorry if I startled you,' he said in a gravelly voice that carried an American accent. 'Am I right in guessing that you're Selina Carr?'

'I am.'

She looked around for Alora and was relieved to see the girl hurrying towards them.

'I'm Hank Wayne, Miss Carr, and I've been somewhat impatiently awaiting your arrival for months. You're certainly a difficult person to locate. I had people in England trying to find you and, despite the fact that they really know their business, they came up with nothing.'

'With a view to buying the plantation, I understand,' she said coldly.

'Ah! You've been told about me!'

He smiled but there was no amusement in his voice and his dark eyes remained watchful, like a bird of prey's.

'And you're right. I want to buy you out, lock, stock and barrel.'

The piercing quality of his gaze disconcerted Selina. It seemed to bore right through her, and she suppressed a shiver. This man was completely unemotional, merciless even, and she sensed that he could be a frightening enemy.

'I'm sorry you've gone to so much trouble, Mr Wayne,' she said tensely, 'but I have no intention of selling. In fact I've been looking forward to coming here, and everything I've seen since my arrival has only served to strengthen my intention to remain.'

'Is that so?' He smiled humourlessly. 'Rumour had it that you wouldn't stay on the island, if you ever put in an appearance. So I suspect you're trying to push up the selling price by playing hard to get. Well, that's understandable, but if you do figure on staying here then remember there are places more comfortable to live in than a plantation. I'll pay top-dollar for the place.'

Selina shook her head.

'You sound quite generous, but you're wasting your time, Mr. Wayne.'

A smile touched his lips as he shook his head.

'Time is money, and those two commodities I never waste!'

His voice was pitched low, sounding intense. Dressed in white cotton trousers and a thin, white, short-sleeved shirt he looked comfortably cool, despite the searing heat.

Selina suppressed a sigh.

'I'm afraid you'll find no profit here, Mr Wayne, and I left word at the house that I was not to be disturbed on any account. Paul Clarke, my manager, handles all business, and I believe he has informed you on more than one occasion that the plantation is not for sale.'

'I didn't come from the house, Miss Carr. I knew Clarke would try to prevent me seeing you so I had people watching for your arrival so I could come directly to you immediately you touched down. It is the only way to do business, and your late arrival on the scene after your father's death has

41

made this a matter of some urgency.'

'It's a pity your efforts are to no avail.'

'All I'm interested in is the bay itself and enough land on top of the cliff to build a hotel,' he persisted in his harsh tone.

'And ruin my view?' Selina shook her head. 'I wouldn't sell one square inch of this place for all the money in the world. And that is my final word, Mr Wayne, so if you will excuse me!'

She turned to leave.

'I'm quite prepared to deal with your lawyers,' he said quickly. 'Prescott and Renworth in St Honoria. They handled your father's business.'

'How do you know so much about us?'

'There's no mystery about it. With a job this size, no stone is left unturned. I've had a team of specialists working on the project, and they turned in a feasibility study which proves the scheme I envisaged will be profitable. Now, I can see that you're a tough cookie to deal with so I am willing to make some concessions. You can have a rent-free, lifetime lease of a luxury suite on the top floor of the hotel. No problems.'

Selina shook her head, perturbed by this man's persistence.

'I give you full marks for trying, Mr Wayne! But you really are wasting your time.'

She picked up her towel and holdall and walked towards the steps leading up the cliff, but Wayne stepped in front of her. Selina shivered as she met his stony gaze.

'Can we have dinner together?' he demanded. 'I'd like to put my scheme to you in detail. You shouldn't turn it down out of hand. You'd make more from selling to me than you'd ever see in profit from sugar cane.'

'I don't think another meeting between us would serve any useful purpose!' she responded quietly. 'I would be bored by your attempts to change my mind, and you wouldn't enjoy such an unprofitable evening.'

She stepped around him and began to walk up the beach, surprised to find herself trembling. Joanne had called Hank Wayne a forceful man, but obviously that was an understatement for he couldn't take no for an answer.

She walked quickly, her lips compressed, and the sound of his feet in the sand at her back sent a shiver along her spine. The next moment he had grasped her arm, stopping her and stepping in front of her again.

'Look,' he began, but Selina wrenched herself free.

'No, Mr Wayne!' she said firmly. 'This conversation has gone quite far enough, so please stop right there! I've stated that there's no question of selling my property, and I suggest you leave at once.'

Her sharp tone stopped him in his tracks and he gazed at her, a muscle twitching in his left cheek. Selina met his gaze, and his manner suggested that he would ignore her and continue his attempts to persuade her to sell.

'Good morning!' a voice hailed them from behind, and Selina turned her head quickly to see Zack emerging from the sea like a Greek god, shedding droplets of water as he strode to collect his towel from the foot of the palm tree.

Relief filled Selina. Sunlight was glistening on his powerful chest and broad shoulders as he bent to snatch up his towel, which he shook open and draped across one shoulder. She caught her breath and moved away from Wayne, walking towards Zack.

'I thought I was quick off the mark,' Zack observed, his feet swishing in the sand as he approached, 'but you certainly don't let the grass grow under your feet, Wayne.'

His gaze swivelled to Selina and his lips quirked into a smile.

'So now you've met Hank Wayne! Well, you'd better watch out for him. He could eat you alive before breakfast quicker than a great white shark, and you wouldn't know something was wrong until it was too late!'

'Mr Wayne is just leaving.'

Selina fought to control the quiver in her voice as Zack paused at her side. His face was expressionless, but she sensed that he was not feeling the same degree of cheerfulness that had sounded in his voice and his blue eyes were filled with a surprisingly harsh glitter.

'I'll go,' Wayne said. 'But please do consider my offer, Miss Carr.'

His dark gaze drew her eyes, and she shivered, instinctively feeling that here was a man not to be trusted.

'You already have my answer on that, Mr Wayne.'

She was heartened by Zack's presence. Wayne shook his head and departed along the beach.

'Has he been hassling you?' Zack demanded.

'He made a proposition which I rejected out of hand,' she replied, careful to keep her tone even, 'and if you're here with the same intention, then you're also wasting your time.'

'Me?' He smiled lazily. 'I'm merely taking my morning swim. I've been doing it for years now, and I don't see why I should break the habit because the plantation has a new boss.'

'I thought this is a private beach.'

'So did I, but Hank Wayne was here.'

'He was trespassing.'

Selina was faintly irritated by Zack's self assurance, despite her relief at his presence.

'Well, I'm not! I was given permission to swim here.'

'By whom? Paul?'

'No. By your father, as it happens.'

'Oh.' She frowned. 'And do you come ten miles every morning just to swim in the bay?'

'I have been a bit remiss in the past, but if you'll be swimming regularly at this time then I'll be here every morning in future. You're a very charming addition to the scenery!'

He smiled, and Selina, aware of the direction of his eyes, pulled the beach cloak tightly around her slender body, noting that his manner had changed considerably from the day before. Was this what he had termed 'working on her?' She suppressed a shiver of awareness that he, too, wanted to buy the plantation.

'If Father let you swim here then I have no wish to deny you,' she said. 'But we'll arrange your visits so we don't clash. I like privacy!'

She turned to walk rather unsteadily towards the cliff steps and did not look back. Reaching the steps, she climbed more quickly than she should have, and was breathless long before she reached the top, but she forced herself to go on. She paused on the top step and looked down into the bay, expecting to see Zack on the beach, but he was swimming again, heading once more for the reef.

'Isn't it dangerous swimming that far out, Alora?' she demanded.

'Not for a man like Mr Zack!' the girl retorted.

They returned to the house and Selina found Joanne on the veranda, seated at a small desk, writing busily. She looked up and smiled, looking cool despite the heat of the morning.

'Did you enjoy your swim?' she enquired.

Selina explained what had occurred and saw a shadow cross Joanne's face.

'It was fortunate Zack was there,' she observed. 'It's strange how Zack and Wayne never hit it off, but that's probably because they're both after the same thing, although they want it for totally different reasons. We're all members of the yacht club at St Honoria, along the coast, and Zack disliked Wayne the moment he showed his face there.'

'I should think it's quite easy to dislike Mr Wayne,' Selina observed, recalling the man's dominating manner.

'And all too easy to like Zack,' Joanne countered.

'Really? Well, I have no intention of falling under his spell,' Selina said firmly. 'How often does he swim in the bay?'

'I haven't seen him over this way in weeks. Once he was always visiting, and I used to wonder how he managed to do his work.'

'So he drove all the way over here this morning just to take a swim?'

Joanne smiled.

'No matter what you might think, Zack works hard, and he has the best interests of the island at heart.'

'Is he married?'

'No. He was engaged once. Diane came from England. She stayed for a few months but left suddenly and never returned. Zack has never said anything about that episode in his life, but I suspect it was quite painful, although he's getting over it now. Would you like a drink? You must be parched after your exertions.'

'Not at the moment, thanks. I'll change first.' Selina paused. 'I've been thinking. I'll have to find a worthwhile occupation here. I can't live as if I'm perpetually on holiday because I would lose all sense of purpose in life. How do you occupy your days, Joanne?'

'I've always found a great deal to do. And now you've arrived I must begin to think of moving back to my own house. Paul thought you shouldn't be left on your own until you've settled in, especially with Hank Wayne around. Later, I'll introduce you to people, and you must certainly become a member of the yacht club.'

'I'm afraid I don't know anything about yachting!'

'Then you must learn. Your father's yacht, *Trade Wind*, is moored in the yacht basin at St Honoria.'

'Father's yacht!' Selina was astounded. 'Joanne, you'd better tell me exactly what I have inherited.'

'Didn't your solicitors in London tell you anything?'

'They did, but I wasn't in a fit state to take it all in at the time.'

'Your father's solicitors here were Prescott and Renworth in St Honoria.

Why don't you see them?'

'I will!' Selina nodded. 'But right now I must shower and change.'

She went up to her room and stripped off her bikini to step into the shower, her thoughts whirling. A pang stabbed through her when she relived the tense encounter with Hank Wayne and recalled her relief at Zack's appearance.

Drying herself, she donned a button-through denim skirt and a shirt which was wide and loose and could do duty as a jacket. She pushed her feet into dress sandals and slipped a gold bracelet on her left wrist. Checking her appearance in a tall mirror, she was pleased with the reflection that gazed back at her. She dabbed perfume on both wrists before leaving the room. In the back of her mind, she wondered when she would see Zack again.

Descending the stairs, Selina frowned when she heard a man's voice coming from the veranda, and her heart missed a beat when she suspected that Hank

Wayne might have followed her from the beach. She paused, her pulses racing, then steeled herself, drew a deep breath and went out to the veranda. There she stopped in mid-stride, for Zack was sitting with Joanne, who arose to fetch more coffee.

Zack got to his feet, smiling, his blue eyes matching swords with Selina's narrowed gaze.

'Your morning swim has done something for you,' he remarked. 'And the scenery has definitely improved with your arrival!'

'When do you manage to get any work done?' she queried rather icily.

He smiled, ignoring her question, and Joanne reappeared before he could reply.

'I was saying to Zack that you'll need someone to introduce you to his circle of friends on the island,' Joanne said cheerfully.

Then she paused and a frown crossed her face as if she sensed an atmosphere. But she shrugged and plunged on.

'I don't mix with that fast set personally, but Zack is one of its leaders, and it would give him something to do to show you around.'

'Thank you, but I'm a girl who likes to find her own landmarks.'

Selina refused to meet Zack's gaze, although she could feel his presence insistently demanding her attention.

'I need to get to know people fairly well before I can even consider making friends.'

'Quite right, too,' Zack commented, 'considering some of the people about these days!'

He grimaced when Selina met his gaze and she sensed his mockery. She drew a deep breath, a perverse thought filling her mind. His arrogance was such that if she decided she could not live here on Tarango, Zack Halliday was the last man she would consider selling to, and Hank Wayne would never get the chance to buy!

3

'It may be too soon to throw Selina in at the deep end,' Zack observed drily. 'Of course, I'm willing to introduce her to my circle of friends, but I wouldn't want to be accused of trying to worm myself into her good books in order to get this place if she does sell out.'

'I'm not ready yet to plunge into local society,' Selina demurred. 'I'm going to acclimatise gradually and live quietly.'

Zack rose to take his leave and Selina, looking at Joanne, became aware that the woman was watching her closely. These two were apparently in league in some kind of action that had been planned, Selina could tell, and wondered if it was merely to buy the plantation and preserve it should it come on the market.

'Is Zack giving you a hard time?'

Joanne asked when he'd gone.

'He's in no position to do that, and being my neighbour doesn't give him any privileges over anyone else, whatever understanding he may have had with my father. But I am at a loss to account for the general assumption that I will sell up at the earliest possible moment.'

'It's the fact that you didn't put in an appearance immediately after your father died,' Joanne said softly. 'But I'm sure people will change their minds when they get to know you.'

Selina was aware that her nerves were on edge after the meeting with Hank Wayne, and she felt uncomfortably restless as she finished her coffee. She had been looking forward to a quiet time in which to get to know her surroundings and slip gently into the new life she had planned for herself, but here she was encumbered by intrigue.

'Is there a car on the estate I can use?' she asked Joanne.

'Certainly. Until you get a car of your own you can use mine.'

Joanne fetched a keyring out of her handbag and held it out.

'Thanks,' Selina said. 'I'll drive into Saint Honoria. I must visit the solicitors to learn exactly what I've let myself in for here. Once I'm sure of my ground, I'll be able to start planning my future.'

'Start as you mean to go on,' Joanne advised, 'and don't let anyone take advantage of you.'

'You sound like a mother,' Selina replied, smiling, then she frowned, for her mother had never been like that . . .

It was pleasant to drive into town, Selina discovered, as she followed the winding road along the top of the cliffs, completely absorbed by her exotic surroundings. She could hardly believe that she had finally arrived in this tropical paradise, and when she reached a sharp bend in the road and saw a lay-by on the cliff overlooking the scintillating bay, she pulled into it and switched off the engine.

A sigh of contentment escaped her as she gazed out over the bay.

She heaved a long sigh of appreciation and tried to steady her racing thoughts. She was excited by her arrival here, and yet the present situation at the plantation did much to dampen her enthusiasm. Zack certainly had an attitude towards her, although she could understand his motives. He was afraid she would sell the plantation to Hank Wayne, who would spoil the island with his ideas for development.

Yet she had told Zack that he had nothing to fear. But he had apparently decided before she arrived that she would sell out at the first opportunity and return to England, although that attitude could have been born of his unfortunate experience with the English girl he had planned to marry.

Perhaps Zack's manner could be overlooked. Then her expression hardened. Hank Wayne, however, was a serious threat to her peace of mind. His manner perturbed her, and his initial insistence warned that she could expect him to reappear again to continue his persuasion.

But she had no intention of selling out, and sighed as she prepared to go on. She started up the engine again, took a last look at the bay, then checked the rear view mirror before pulling out on to the narrow road. She got back on to the road and accelerated, when suddenly, as if from nowhere, there was a huge sugar cane truck behind her, lights flashing and horn blaring as it bore down upon her.

Selina frowned as she looked in the mirror, recalling the truck that had passed them when Zack first drove her home. Zack had slowed and pulled into the side to permit the larger vehicle to pass. She immediately slowed and drew well into the side of the road. The truck sped by so close to her that Selina caught her breath as the car rocked. She feared the worst and pulled in even closer to the grass verge. The truck hammered by, horn blaring, with barely inches between them. The nearside front wheel of the car struck the verge and mounted it, the impact ripping the steering-wheel from Selina's grasp as she hit rough, uneven ground.

She slammed her foot on the brake as the car bumped and lurched out of control off the road. The cliff edge seemed to race towards her and she spun the steering-wheel frantically. Then a front wheel caught in a hole in the cliff top and the car lurched to a halt. Suddenly, she was thrown sideways, her head thudding against the side window. She was dazed, frighteningly aware that the front of the car was only a foot from the edge of the cliff and the drop of two hundred feet or so below.

Thrusting open the door, Selina tumbled out of the car and staggered away from it. She could still hear the horn of the truck blaring in the distance, but the big vehicle had already disappeared from sight around a bend.

She gasped and sank to the ground to collect her wits.

What a maniac! She couldn't believe anyone would drive so criminally fast on such a narrow road. She looked both ways along the road, which was now deserted and still, and drew a deep breath to steady her ruffled nerves.

By degrees her senses returned and she rose to take stock of the situation. Returning to the car, she saw how close it was to the edge of the cliff and froze in horror. If she hadn't slowed the instant she saw the truck coming up from behind she would have gone over the edge of the cliff! She caught her breath, heart pounding. She had had a very narrow escape!

Getting into the car, she started the engine and backed off the verge, checking the road for other vehicles as she did so. Her hands were trembling as she continued on her way, gripped by shock. Her head was aching, and when she touched her temple, where it had struck the window, she felt the stickiness of blood and glanced at her reflection in the rear view mirror. A small trickle of blood was oozing from a darkening bruise on her right temple. She felt faint from shock as she drove on.

St Honoria nestled in a fold in the cliffs, and Selina was relieved when she reached it. She found the heat intolerable the moment she stepped out of the car and realised, as she walked unsteadily along the main street, that she would have to take things easy until she became acclimatised. She saw a brass plate proclaiming the offices of Prescott and Renworth, Solicitors. She entered the building and was confronted by a young woman typing at a desk.

'Can I help you?' the girl asked.

'I'm Selina Carr. I'd like to see the person who handled my father's affairs.'

At that moment, a door opposite was opened and two men emerged, chatting together, from the office beyond. Selina was surprised to see that the first was

Zack Halliday. He paused in midstride when he saw her.

'Here already to put your property on the market?' he demanded lightly.

'I like your sense of humour!' she responded.

He laughed, half-turning to his companion.

'Selina Carr, Peter Renworth,' he introduced. 'I'll leave you two together. Take good care of her, Peter. See you this evening at the club.' He smiled at Selina. 'Would you come to join me in the hotel bar across the street when you've settled your business with Peter?' he invited.

'I could certainly do with a cool drink,' she responded, half turning away from him to conceal her injury.

'Fine! I'll be expecting you!' His keen gaze studied her for a moment before he turned away.

'I'm pleased to meet you, Miss Carr,' Peter Renworth interrupted, holding out his hand. 'How can I help you?'

Selina shook hands.

'Please forgive me dropping in unannounced but I'm anxious to know exactly what I've inherited. I've no idea. Can you fill me in on the details?'

'Certainly! There's a copy of your father's will on file. If you'll step into my office.'

He turned to the door and ushered her into a room with a tall window overlooking the bay.

'Please, sit down, and if you'll excuse me I'll get your father's file.'

He departed, and Selina turned to look at the law books closely packed on shelves in the office. But they were of no interest to her and she glanced at the burdened desk, her eyes narrowing when she read Hank Wayne's name on a file. So Prescott and Renworth were also acting for the redoubtable American property developer!

She had just turned her attention back to the view from the window when Renworth returned with a file. He smiled as he met her gaze.

'Now,' he said, opening the file and

extracting a document. 'Everything was quite straightforward. You were named as the sole beneficiary.'

'I was informed of the amount of money left to me and I know of the sugar plantation, but I was told this morning of a yacht I knew nothing about.'

'There is a craft called *Trade Wind*. I can point it out to you from here.'

He crossed to a cupboard for a pair of binoculars and turned to the window.

'If you'll adjust these to your eyes.'

He handed the binoculars to Selina, who focused them.

'Pick out the jetty with the crane on it and look to the left. About halfway along is a white-hulled motor yacht.'

'I see it! There's a name on her stern. *Trade Wind*.'

'She's the fastest craft in these waters,' he said, 'and she's yours! The man you need to see is Bill Sharpley. He runs the yacht marina, and was your father's closest friend for years.'

'Thank you,' Selina said as she lowered the glasses. 'Would you do me a favour? I assume that you are continuing to run the affairs of the plantation.'

'I am, and I'll do whatever I can to help, Miss Carr.'

'Would you let it be known that I have no intention whatsoever of selling the plantation? I'm sure you will be aware of anyone who might be interested in a sale. But Tarango is now my home and I intend to remain here.'

He nodded, his face expressionless.

'Certainly. I'll see to it that the information travels to certain quarters. And if there is anything else I can do to help, then please don't hesitate to contact me.'

'You're very kind,' she responded.

He escorted her to the door and held out his hand, smiling.

'I do hope you will enjoy your life here, Miss Carr. It's a style to which you will have to accustom yourself, but when the magic of the island gets into your blood you'll find it difficult, impossible even, to break away.'

'I won't ever want to leave, I'm sure of it,' she said firmly, and took her leave.

Pausing on the street, she spotted Zack standing in the wide doorway of the hotel opposite. Again she wondered at his motives. If he was merely interested in stopping development on the island then they shared the same sentiments. But until she was sure of him she had to be careful.

He lifted a hand and waved, and she glanced both ways along the street before crossing, her gaze intent on his smiling face.

'That didn't take long,' he observed, backing into the lobby of the hotel as she entered.

'There were a few details of my father's will I needed to get straight,' she explained. 'And I've just learned that I have inherited a yacht.'

'*Trade Wind* — and that's a boat and a half! I've always been interested in her but your father wouldn't sell, even when he became too ill to take her out. Do you sail?'

'I've never had the opportunity.'

'Then may I be permitted to take you out for a sail? I always wanted to get my hands on your father's yacht.'

'The yacht as well as the plantation!' she observed tartly.

He glanced at her keenly, then smiled and nodded.

'I want the plantation in order to preserve it,' he said. 'But the boat I'd like purely for pleasure.'

'When can you take me out in her?'

'There's no time like the present! But the yacht has been idle for some time, although Bill Sharpley will have kept her seaworthy. We'd better take a look at her before I commit myself.'

Selina nodded as they sat down at a table. She ordered a cold drink, and sat listening to Zack's polite conversation. But she was keyed up. Her pulses were racing and there was a pain in her temple. She fingered the bruise and

Zack suddenly noticed her condition.

'You're looking pale,' he observed with a frown. 'Are you feeling the effects of the sun?'

She decided to explain what had happened on the road and saw his eyes narrow. He examined her temple, his fingers gentle.

'This is terrible! You might have been killed! And the driver didn't stop? Did you get the number of the truck?'

'It all happened too fast for me to notice anything,' she protested.

'What time did it happen? I'll find out who was driving towards town. It has to be one of the drivers from your estate. I'll talk to Paul. That maniac has got to be stopped before he kills someone. He passed us yesterday when I was driving you home, if you remember.'

'I do,' she responded. 'But I'm not hurt so there's no harm done.'

'Do you feel well enough to make a boat trip? If we can take out *Trade Wind* we'll be gone several hours. Had you planned anything else for today?'

'Nothing, and I think a boat trip will soothe my nerves. But if we're to be away for hours then I'd better inform Joanne.'

He nodded and indicated a public telephone in the lobby. Selina called Joanne and informed her of her plans. When she returned to Zack, he led her from the hotel.

'You're not really suitably dressed for a long sea trip, but you'll do for a sail round the bay and a run through the reef. We can let *Trade Wind* show you her paces today and make a longer trip another time.'

'Whatever you say,' Selina agreed. 'It sounds like great fun.'

'But are you a good sailor?'

He was now leading her through an alley to the quay.

'I don't know. I've never been on a small boat before.'

'Then you're in for a treat. If I could, I'd spend all my days afloat.'

They reached the quay and Selina

looked out across the bay. The water was calm, but farther out she could see white water and huge waves marking the reef.

'Do we have to go out through that choppy stuff?' she asked.

'There's no other way to reach the open sea!' He laughed. 'You'll soon find out if you're a good sailor or not.'

'Isn't it dangerous? It looks very rough to me!'

'It's not as bad as it looks, so long as you know what you're doing!'

He took hold of her arm and they followed the quay to the yacht marina. Selina could see the yacht at her mooring, and her pulses quickened as she thought of her father.

'We must have a word with Bill Sharpley,' Zack observed. 'But if I know Bill, *Trade Wind* will be ready to sail at a moment's notice.'

And so it proved. Sharpley, a wizened, little man, in his sixties, with rough-hewn features and skin the colour of burnished copper, greeted

Selina like an old friend.

'I'm happy to meet you,' he said. 'Your father and I were close friends for more years than I care to remember, and I knew him better than anyone on the island. He talked about you all the time, right to the end, and it was a tragedy that you never came to see him.'

'I wish I could have!' Selina sighed. 'Mother never talked about Father. She always said he had died before I was born. It wasn't until she was dying recently that she told me the truth, and I was devastated to learn that Father had died only three years ago!'

Sharpley looked keenly at her, then nodded.

'I guess that is the way your mother would act. She was an intense woman.'

'Is *Trade Wind* ready for sea?' Zack cut in.

'She's always ready,' Sharpley replied. 'Her fuel tanks are topped up.'

'Fuel tanks? Has *Trade Wind* got an engine?' Selina demanded.

'She certainly has. She's a motor

yacht, built in my boatyard.'

Pride sounded in Sharpley's tone.

'Are you going to take her out?' he asked.

'We want to see if Selina has what it takes to be a sailor!' Zack replied.

Zack smiled at her over Sharpley's head as he spoke.

'If she's anything like her father, then she'll take to it like a duck to water,' Sharpley replied. 'And you couldn't have a better sailor than Zack to crew for you, Selina. I was always the best, but I've got too old to hang on to that title and Zack has taken it over.'

Zack took hold of Selina's arm.

'Come along,' he said impatiently. 'You can have a yarn with Bill another time. We've got a boat to take out.'

They walked along the jetty between two lines of moored craft and Selina narrowed her eyes against the glare of the sun. She could now see *Trade Wind* at closer quarters, and could tell, even through her inexperienced eyes, that the yacht was in first-class condition.

The paintwork was gleaming and the narrow deck was clean and tidy. There was a tall main-mast with a furled sail, and a long boom reached back over the cockpit to the stern.

'The deck is solid teak,' Zack said. 'Bill used only the best materials in her. Come aboard! If ships have instincts, then *Trade Wind* will know you are related to it's previous owner.'

Emotion constricted Selina's throat as she stepped aboard the craft. Zack showed her around with the air of one who was quite familiar with his surroundings. There were two large cabins, a small shower room, and a well equipped galley.

'She's rigged so one person can sail her,' he explained. 'If you find you like sailing, then I'll give you lessons in seamanship and navigation, but you'll have no problem handling her on the engine, although you'll need a great deal of experience before you can take her through the gap in the reef out there.'

Selina nodded, aware that for the first time since they'd met, his tone was perfectly normal because he was deeply interested in this particular subject. She sat in the cockpit while he started the engine, cast off and got under way.

A cool breeze fanned her face, and she experienced a sense of well-being. She watched Zack, noting that he handled the craft expertly, and as they moved across the bay, he stood at the helm, controlling their passage, his expression intent, his profile sharply defined by the brilliant sun. He was certainly a handsome man, she decided, studying him.

'This is most enjoyable,' she observed. 'But the bay is calm, and I dread to think what it will be like when we get farther out.'

'Don't worry about it. You can sit where you are when we negotiate the gap. Just hang on to that stanchion beside you and don't let go. It won't be as bad as it looks so don't worry. You'll be quite safe.'

Selina nodded. She peered ahead, watching the white water farther out, where huge rollers were crashing on the reef. She could see no break in the surf and steeled herself. Already the smooth surface of the bay was becoming agitated, and she realised that the effect of the waves was beginning to reach them.

'Where is the gap you mentioned?'

She had to raise her voice above the booming roar of the surf in order to be heard.

'It was there the last time I came this way,' he countered with a smile, his blue eyes gleaming. 'Don't worry! I know it's an awesome sight. I've never forgotten my first trip through. But you're in good hands, so sit back and enjoy it.'

Selina nodded and grasped the stanchion. The craft began to roll like a living creature as the swell tried to take control. Zack countered by skilful use of the helm, his feet seemingly rooted to the deck as they lurched in a crashing ride through wild water.

Great waves came at them from all sides, and she feared they would be overwhelmed. But Zack was intent on steering, and she could only admire the way he mastered the surging water. Then they were through the gap and running to calmer sea beyond.

'There you are!'

He was grinning like a schoolboy.

'That's your first time behind you. It wasn't so bad, was it?'

'It was terrifying but I loved every moment of it! How on earth did you learn to steer like that? It must have taken years to gain the experience necessary to negotiate such a stretch of water, to say nothing of nerve!'

'It's merely a matter of holding the craft in the centre of the gap and letting the engine take you. There are a couple of spots where you have to fight against the waves, but it's not difficult if the engine is powerful enough to fight the current. I'll teach you to do it.'

'I don't think I'd ever be able to

master it, but I'd certainly like to try.'

'It's actually easier going the other way,' he observed. 'So when we come back, you can have your first lesson.'

'I'll look forward to it.'

She drew a deep breath, keenly aware of his nearness, her exhilaration having taken her close to him. He was looking at her intently, exuding a magnetism that tugged at her senses. She looked away from him as he shifted his gaze to survey the horizon.

'This craft moves like a dream,' he remarked. 'If you discover that you don't like sailing and want to sell, please give me the first offer!'

'Plus the first offer on the plantation,' she observed drily. 'What's the name of that island over there?'

Her attention was attracted by a smudge on the horizon.

'St Osyth. It's uninhabited, but it has a secluded cove that's perfect for swimming. Would you like to see it from close quarters? We won't be going much farther today.'

'Fine!'

She was elated after the excitement of negotiating the reef and filled with a yearning for adventure.

'I'm in your hands.'

He smiled and she shivered. Being alone with him in this expanse of blue sea was almost too much for her romantic soul. The spell of the tropics and the seascape was affecting her, indicating that her inhibitions had been left back in England.

This was another world, and she had imperceptibly changed from the heart-broken girl who had set out from England only days ago with the intention of building herself a new life among strangers. But here were all the ingredients for change, right down to this attractive man who had come into her life.

She glanced at Zack, saw he was regarding her intently, as if able to read her thoughts, and heat rushed to her cheeks. But he smiled and waved a casual hand at their surroundings.

'You haven't seen anything like this before, have you?' he asked.

'Never! I haven't been here five minutes but already I'm hooked!'

He studied her, then laughed and shook his head.

'So long as the island isn't developed,' he said. 'You may be wondering why I'm so set against the development being planned by Hank Wayne, but similar development has been carried out on some of the larger islands in this area and it has ruined them, destroyed their character and spoiled the environment.'

She met his gaze, saw the fire in his eyes, and suppressed a shiver. She moistened her lips, but the sudden roar of a powerful engine had Zack whirling away from her and leaping into action. He spun the wheel quickly, swinging them away from the narrow entrance to the cove just ahead.

A low white craft came speeding towards them from the cove, and but for Zack's instinctive action there would have been a collision. Selina watched the smaller craft as it swept around them in a spray-filled half circle before throttling down to come alongside.

A tall, slim young woman climbed aboard the *Trade Wind*. She was dressed only in a white bikini, her long ash-blonde hair blowing free in the breeze, her limbs sun-bronzed. Selina watched in amazement as the girl threw herself into Zack's arms and kissed him passionately on the lips before turning her head to look at Selina.

Zack was smiling, albeit a trifle grimly, Selina noticed, his hands instinctively lifting to grasp the woman's slender, tanned body.

'Fiona, one of these days your recklessness will cause serious trouble for someone!' he said firmly. 'You know better than to emerge from the cove like that!'

'How was I to know you were approaching?' she countered. 'Don't be angry with me, Zack! You don't know how I've missed you this past month.'

'Missed me! You're the one who couldn't wait to get to Europe on holiday!'

He sighed and let his hands fall away from her. Fiona half turned her head to look at Selina.

'Hi,' she greeted. 'I'm Fiona Stuart, and you must be Selina Carr. I've heard so much about you. There's been a great deal of speculation about you. And you haven't wasted any time, Zack!'

She laughed, her eyes filling with fire.

'Watch your step with him, Selina! He's a charmer, and if a girl has something he wants then he usually gets it.'

Zack shrugged and smiled when he met Selina's gaze.

'You've been warned!' he said, then turned abruptly to grasp the wheel, for the tide was edging them in closer to the cove. 'Get your boat away, Fiona,' he ordered.

'I just had to say hello,' Fiona

responded. 'I'll call you in a day or two, Selina, and we'll arrange to meet. Zack seems to have taken you under his wing, but you'll need more perspective than he'll give you. 'Bye for now!'

Selina opened her mouth to reply but Fiona stepped over the side of the yacht into her own boat, and the next instant the roar of a powerful marine engine shattered the silence as the speedboat shot away to carve a swathe of foam and spray on its race to the distant horizon. Selina heaved a sigh.

'That was Fiona, that was!' Zack said. 'And with young Tom Bessemer in tow! She's been in Europe on holiday for the past month and I hadn't heard she was back.'

He returned his attention to taking the yacht into the cove. Selina was conscious of disappointment, realising that Fiona's words had aroused a confusion of suspicion in her mind about Zack's real intentions. She drew a deep breath and made a mental note to be more careful in future, both with what she said and how she acted.

But she was aware, in that illuminating moment, that some of her pleasure at being in Zack's company had mysteriously evaporated because of Fiona's existence.

4

The isle of St Osyth was volcanic, bleak and craggy, and when Zack edged the yacht into the cove, Selina was impressed by its stark beauty. The high cliffs surrounding the cove were the habitat of seabirds, and as the echoes of the engine were flung around the rocky ledges a countless number of birds took off from their roosts and flew over the boat.

'This is beautiful.' Selina sighed with pleasure. 'But doesn't coming here disturb the birds? This place should be a sanctuary.'

'They're quite accustomed to the boats that put in.'

Zack edged the craft closer to a rock and craned sideways, checking that the fenders were in position to protect the hull. He switched off the engine, hastened to the bows to pick up a small anchor that was attached to a thick rope and sprang on to the rock and wedged the anchor in a crevice.

The echoes of the engine died away and silence fell. Selina surveyed her surroundings. The air echoed with the haunting cries of seabirds. Zack had now disappeared through the hatch into the cabin area, to return with a pair of powerful binoculars which he handed to her. She focused the glasses and gazed around with interest, but with Zack's diverting presence she found it hard to concentrate, and risked a glance at him. He smiled.

His face was highlighted by the glare of the sun, its classic lines stark and firm, and the keen expression in his eyes held her attention so strongly that she had to make an effort to look away. She raised the glasses to her eyes once more and scanned the cliffs. While her attention was fixed upon the scenery, she became aware of Zack moving closer until her nerves protested with a warning that alerted her defences.

'We'd better start back to St Honoria!' he observed. 'I didn't think we would be this late.'

'I'm in no hurry!' she said instantly.

He smiled.

'Unfortunately, I have some business in town and must be back there before the afternoon ends.'

'Very well!'

Selina wondered if his business had to do with Fiona.

He turned away to retrieve the anchor, and Selina sat in the stern and watched his movements, disappointed because the trip was ending. The sea miles slipped by, and all too soon Tarango came up over the sparkling horizon. Selina found the return through the reef as exhilarating as the trip out, and clung to the convenient stanchion while the yacht was whirled through the white water that raged and roared around them.

Then they were through the gap and gliding into the calm water of the bay. She looked at Zack with respect as he took the yacht neatly in against the jetty from which they had set out.

'I need food or I shall collapse from hunger,' she said as they reached the street once the yacht was safely moored.

They entered the hotel they'd been in earlier, and had a meal together. Selina sighed with relief once she'd eaten.

'I can't remember feeling more hungry,' she observed.

'It's the combination of sea air and climate,' he said. 'And I suspect that you didn't have too much for breakfast, did you?'

'I didn't, but I won't make that mistake again.'

She was unaware that the sun streaming through a nearby window was glinting on her hair, creating a red-gold halo around her face.

'I've had a most enjoyable time! But now I'd better go home,' she added.

'Be careful how you drive!' he warned, and Selina suppressed a shiver. 'I could drive you any other time,' he offered, then paused and added, 'Would you like me to drive behind you to your place, just in case?'

'In case of what?' she demanded. 'Do you think there was something more sinister to that incident this morning?'

'I didn't say that,' he countered.

'But if you think it then there must be something more in your mind,' she persisted. 'Do you think there was more to it than just a careless truck driver?'

'No! I know that truck driver by sight, and he's a regular road hog. I wouldn't trust him with a bicycle, let alone a vehicle. Any time you see him on the road, give him a wide berth.'

'If he works for me then I'll see that he doesn't drive again until he has been properly taught to observe the rules of the road,' she said sharply. 'Thank you for taking me out in the yacht.'

'It was my pleasure,' he replied with a smile.

Selina was still frowning when they reached the street, and she pointed out Joanne's car. He waited as she slid into the driving seat, then closed the door for her. She drove off, glancing in the mirror for a final look at him.

He was standing on the pavement, and Selina was startled when a girl suddenly appeared at his side and took hold of his arm. Selina recognised her as Fiona, just before the car turned a corner and she lost sight of them.

She frowned as she left St Honoria. Driving back to the estate, she had time to reflect on her experiences, and was aware that Zack had made an impact on her. She hadn't been so attracted to a man before, and despite Fiona's arrival on the scene, she was more than anxious to see him again.

She drove carefully despite her thoughts, watching the road ahead and behind for trouble, suspicious of every passing vehicle. But the journey passed without incident and she was relieved when she drew up in front of the house. Joanne was relaxing on the veranda, and she smiled as Selina flopped down in an easy chair beside her.

'When you phoned to say you were going out in the yacht with Zack, I didn't expect you back until dark,' Joanne observed. 'Did you enjoy yourself?'

'I did indeed!'

Selina recounted her experiences, but when she mentioned Fiona Stuart she saw Joanne frown.

'So she's back! I was under the impression she had gone for good. She's besotted with Zack, and chased him brazenly for months before her father sent her to Europe. How Zack tolerates her is a mystery to me, but he has business interests with her father. He owns a sugar-cane plantation on the other side of the island, so that must be the reason why he suffers her attentions.'

Selina nodded. She had seen that Fiona was a pushy type, but the easy familiarity between Zack and the girl hinted at a deeper level of intimacy, and she was thoughtful when she went to her room to shower and change.

Later, she sat on the veranda waiting for Zack to arrive, but when the sun went down and there was no sign of him, she began to suspect that Fiona had caused him to change his mind.

Paul arrived home, looking tired after his day's work, and Selina felt guilty at her own leisurely day. When he sat down to chat, Selina mentioned her skirmish with the sugar cane truck that morning.

'What time would that be?' he demanded, frowning, and shook his head when she told him. 'That truck was stolen from headquarters this morning. A joy-rider, we suspect. It was found this afternoon, piled up in a ravine. There were footprints around the wreckage but no other clues. I think you were very lucky this morning. The idiot driving the truck might have put you over the cliff.'

'I was only a few inches from the edge.'

'And you have a nasty bruise,' he observed. 'You're lucky to be alive.

These joy-riders have become quite a problem on the island. A number of people have been killed by being in the wrong place at the wrong time. I'll inform the police what happened to you. Did you get a look at the driver?'

She shook her head.

'It all happened so quickly, and the sun was shining on the truck's wind-screen.'

Joanne called Paul to his meal, and, left alone, Selina realised that she was restless because of Zack's non-appearance. Sitting on the veranda, she could feel pressure building up in her mind. She decided to go into town in the hope of seeing Zack. She informed Joanne of her intention, despite her misgivings at being alone on the road. But nothing happened and she arrived safely in the town.

Entering the now familiar hotel, she regretted her impulse the moment she saw Zack in the bar with Fiona. She turned quickly to leave before he could see her and almost collided with a burly figure entering silently behind her. She stifled a gasp when she found herself looking into the face of none other than Hank Wayne.

'Good evening, Miss Carr. It's a pleasure to see you,' he greeted. 'May I buy you a drink?'

He smiled but his expression did not soften, and his eyes were hard and bright.

'I'm not trespassing now, and I'd like an opportunity to talk to you.'

'Thank you but I'm late for an appointment,' she replied unhesitatingly, 'and as my place is not on the market, a business chat would be a complete waste of your time.'

'I'd still like to put my side of the deal to you,' he persisted.

'There's no chance that you could change my mind about selling.'

Selina shook her head, somewhat surprised by his doggedness.

'At the beach you said time was money and you never wasted either. But evidently you are prepared to spoil a beautiful evening on a lost cause. I'm sure you must have done your homework on me, and realise that I won't sell under any circumstance.'

'Everything can be sold,' he retorted. 'And everyone has a selling price. All we have to do is find your level.'

'Ah, there you are!'

Zack spoke quietly at her back, and Selina was relieved as he stepped to her side.

'I was beginning to think you weren't coming!'

She drew a deep breath, smiling, trying to appear casual.

'Sorry I'm late. I was talking business with Paul. We're getting to grips with what needs doing to the plantation to bring it up to date.'

She looked pointedly at Wayne.

'You see, far from thinking of selling, I'm prepared to develop the plantation in other ways.'

Wayne's eyes were bright as a vulture's and remained inscrutable as he smiled and nodded.

'Very well, Miss Carr, I know when I'm beaten. I shall withdraw gracefully from the scene, and I wish you success in your new life.'

'Thank you, Mr Wayne.'

She sighed with relief, but there was mistrust in her mind as he departed.

'It looks as if you've put him in his place,' Zack observed. 'I got a shock when I glanced round and saw him confronting you. He must be watching your movements very closely in order to pounce on you whenever you're alone. And don't underestimate him! I've heard some nasty tales about his business methods.'

'He's certainly tenacious! I thought I'd made it quite clear this morning that I had no intention of selling, but he doesn't take no for an answer. What have I got to do to convince him that I'm here to stay?'

'Put him out of your mind.'

Zack's face was grim as he looked into her eyes.

'If he bothers you again then let me

know and I'll have a quiet word with him. What are your plans now? I intended calling on you but was held up in town with some pressing business, and now I'm caught up with Fiona. But come and join us. I wanted to see you but I wouldn't drag Fiona along with me.'

So that was why he had failed to turn up! Selina sighed, recalling that Joanne said that Fiona had run after him shamelessly.

'Help me out,' he said urgently. 'Come along.'

Selina accompanied him, and the jealousy which appeared in Fiona's blue eyes at the sight of her smote Selina like the edge of a sword as Zack pulled out a seat opposite the girl. Selina smiled, although she wanted to leave when she appreciated the depth of Fiona's emotions, and began to wish she had curbed the impulse that had brought her into town.

'Hello, Fiona! I like your dress!' she

said lightly. 'Did you buy it in Europe?'

The girl glanced down at her dress and shrugged.

'Paris. I wish I were still on holiday. I didn't want to come back, but here I am, and still stifled by the petty restrictions of island life. I wish I were in your shoes.'

She regarded Selina with an expressionless gaze.

'If you didn't want to live here, you could leave at a moment's notice and no-one would get upset. But you're talking of staying on when any sane female wouldn't come within a thousand miles of the place.'

Zack sat down between them, his forearms resting on the table. He didn't appear to be listening to their conversation, but looked around until he caught a waiter's eye and raised an imperious finger.

'What would you like to drink, Selina?' he asked.

'Something cool and pleasant, please,' she replied.

'I'll have another Pink Volcano,' Fiona said.

'No, you won't!' Zack said abruptly. 'You've had enough to drink, and if you want any more, you'll have to buy it yourself. I don't want your father blaming me for your excesses now that you're back. We've finished with the way things were before you went to Europe.'

Fiona glared at him, shaking her head like a wilful child.

'How do you occupy your time on the island, Fiona?' Selina inquired, trying to ignore the apparent situation that existed between these two. 'I've just arrived, and already I'm wondering how to fill in the hours.'

'Fiona doesn't do anything,' Zack cut in. 'Her life is one long round of pleasure-seeking, and if you hope to do anything constructive, Selina, then you'd do well to remain outside the influence of her set.'

'You're so kind!'

Fiona snatched up her handbag, her

eyes glinting as she looked at Selina.

'You'll soon learn whom to avoid round here if you want a good time! And I wish you luck because you'll certainly need it. Good-night!'

She whirled to depart, and Selina frowned. Zack met her gaze and shook his head. Just then, the waiter approached and Selina watched Zack intently, wondering what kind of a man he really was. He seemed to treat Fiona with contempt. But the girl was apparently making a nuisance of herself and he had obviously hit upon the right note to keep her under control and at arm's length.

She watched Fiona cross the room to a corner table and speak to Hank Wayne, who got to his feet with a smile and drew out a chair for her to sit down.

'I've warned Fiona to stay away from Wayne,' Zack observed. 'But she's so obstinate, and completely regardless of consequences.'

The waiter brought their drinks, but Selina kept her attention on Fiona and

Hank Wayne. There was another man at Wayne's table, and she soon realised that he was watching her intently. Whenever she looked in his direction, he was gazing at her, and finally she moved her chair slightly to face another direction.

'What's wrong?' Zack demanded.

'The man with Hank Wayne and Fiona keeps staring at me,' she responded.

'That's Pete Brewer, Wayne's field man. He's a glorified errand boy, and handles any problems that Wayne comes up against.'

'And am I one of Wayne's problems?' Selina demanded, and a pang stabbed through her as she considered the implications of such a situation.

'You've certainly put a dent in his plans,' Zack said seriously. 'He's wasted a lot of time on his project here because he couldn't negotiate with you, and time is money to a man like Wayne, as he's forever telling people.'

'I've already heard that side of his

philosophy,' Selina observed, and dismissed Wayne from her thoughts. 'Can we get out of here? I feel a need for fresh air!'

Zack nodded and they left the hotel.

'Are you all right?' His voice cut through her thoughts as they strolled along. 'I asked a question and you were miles away. Is something worrying you?'

'No. I'm merely reflective. Everything is new to me at the moment, and I have so much to think about. What was your question?'

'Would you like to take a walk along the cliffs? I don't think you'd appreciate the casino, or my circle of friends.'

'I'd love to walk,' she responded.

'And are you suitably shod?' he teased, looking down at her feet.

'If the ground isn't too rough.'

'There's a path along the top of the cliffs. It'll be dark in about two hours, and that should be about right.'

Selina nodded as she stepped out beside him. He drew her like a magnet, and she was keenly aware of her reaction to him.

They walked to the outskirts of St Honoria and then followed the path on to the cliff top that skirted Barracuda Bay. Gazing out across the bay, she felt a sense of tranquillity which was new to her.

She watched as seabirds dived and soared around the cliffs. She glanced at Zack, who was silent, accepting her need to commune with her surroundings in an effort to come to terms with her new way of life. Sensing her gaze, he glanced at her, his blue eyes gleaming in the sunlight of the glorious evening.

They covered a mile at least, and Selina paused by a palm tree to look towards her house on the cliff top. It was stark against the brilliant blue sky beyond, looking no larger than a model, and she realised that her heart was already anchored in it as strongly as if she had always lived there.

'It's a beautiful view,' Zack remarked.

'But can you imagine how it would change if your house was pulled down and a huge glass and stone hotel erected in its place? And the bay! Wayne plans to blast a channel through the reef to make it a safe passage for the tourists he intends should flock here in their thousands. The cane fields would go because he has plans for a golf course, a massive leisure centre, and a much larger yacht marina.'

'And all this would happen if I sold to him?'

'Inevitably!' Zack exclaimed in reply.

'But none of it would occur if I don't.'

'He couldn't put two bricks together!' Zack replied.

'And if I do decide that I can't live here, you're prepared to buy me out to prevent the plantation falling into Wayne's hands.'

'I'm trying to arrange to meet the selling price you would ask.'

'Despite the fact that I am adamant about staying here and running the plantation?' she countered.

'I would be a fool to accept appearances,' he said softly. 'I have to act as if the worst might happen.'

They walked on, and Selina looked at the view inland. Cane fields dominated the foreground then a verdant backdrop of tree-covered ground rose beyond.

'I must get a camera,' she observed.

'I'll show you all the local beauty spots in due course,' he told her.

She gazed out at the reef, reliving those exhilarating moments earlier when he had handled *Trade Wind* so competently in that awesome patch of water. It had been frightening at first, but she had loved the thrilling experience and was keen to encounter it again.

Shadows began to close in and they retraced their steps back along the cliff top, returning to the spot in town where Selina had parked the car.

'You've had a full day today,' he observed. 'Would you like a drink now, or something to eat?'

'No, thanks. I'm feeling very tired. I'll have an early night.'

'Shall I call at your place around eight-thirty in the morning? We could have a swim together.'

'Won't you be busy with Fiona tomorrow?'

She unlocked the car door and slid into the driving seat, smiling when he ignored her question.

'Thank you again for your company today. I can't remember when I enjoyed myself more. It was quite an experience negotiating the gap in the reef.'

'I enjoyed it, too. I'll see you in the morning then!' He smiled. 'We could take the boat out again, too. Good-night.'

'Good-night.'

She closed the door, and as the car moved forward, she glanced round for him but he had already gone from sight. She stifled a sigh, thinking that perhaps he couldn't wait to find Fiona.

She was driving home along the coast road when a car caught her up from behind, its headlights full on, dazzling her. She slowed to allow the vehicle to pass but it remained behind, and much too close for safety.

She had to adjust her rear view mirror to cut down the glare of the headlights, and was relieved when she reached the turn-off to her house. She indicated a right turn but the car behind did not drop back, and she was so afraid of being rammed from behind that she missed her turning and continued along the road. The next instant there was a crash and her car jerked violently as the vehicle behind bumped her.

She almost lost control and swerved across the road. Gripping the steering-wheel, Selina concentrated on driving, her eyes narrowed against the glare enveloping her from behind. The road was unknown to her, and she forced herself to concentrate on driving.

The next bend was sharper than it seemed and she nearly ran off the road.

Tyres screeched as she braked, and again she was struck from behind. Fear encompassed her, but she was angry, too, and looked for a turn-off. She slowed imperceptibly, but the following car rammed her again, trying to force her to maintain speed, and the impact almost threw her across the road.

She gripped the wheel again and drove as she had never driven before, dazzled by the following headlights. Her teeth clenched and fear gripped her as she vowed never to travel alone again.

The car rammed her several times, and Selina was terrified. She came to a straight stretch of road and slowed quickly, then spun the wheel and turned the car. The road was barely wide enough to permit the manoeuvre, and the following car struck her hard. But the impact helped her to turn, and the next instant she was speeding back the way she had come.

The glare of headlights vanished and she sighed with relief when she looked in the mirror and saw the unknown vehicle continuing on its way. She slumped a little, reaction almost rendering her powerless, and relief filled her when she saw her turn-off and she left the main road.

Parking the car at the side of the house, she almost fell out of it in her haste to get clear. Paul stood up on the veranda as she stumbled up the steps towards him. He grasped her and sat her down, and Selina gasped out details of the incident, trembling uncontrollably as reaction caught her.

She cried in relief, and Joanne, drawn by the sound of her voice, appeared and began to soothe her. Selina gulped the strong drink Paul fetched her, and sat watching him when he went to inspect the damage to the car.

It seemed like a nightmare now, but she was deathly afraid. The cane truck that morning had almost run her off the road, and she had been willing to accept that it had been a pure accident. But the driver of that unknown car had been determined to force her off the road, and she trembled uncontrollably as the full impact of what had occurred came home to her. Someone had been trying to kill her!

5

Gradually, Selina's panic subsided, but her ordeal continued. Paul telephoned the police and before long a car arrived with two officers. Selina gave them details of what had happened, but could offer no information about her assailant. She had seen nothing of the other car, having been dazzled by its headlights.

When the policemen examined her car, they found traces of blue paint on the crumpled metal at the rear. They departed, saying they would be in touch later. As Selina watched them drive off, her head was aching, her temples thumping. She decided to go to her room, wanting nothing more than to lie down.

Joanne accompanied her, talking soothingly, but Selina was relieved when she was finally alone. Before getting into bed, she sat on the window sill in the darkness, looking out at the tropical night trying to come to terms with what had happened.

Uppermost in her mind was the suspicion that Hank Wayne was behind the attack on her, but she shook her head in disbelief, unable to accept that he would want to kill her merely for business reasons. She could easily have died had the car gone off the road during those terrifying minutes of the attack.

She hoped the police would be able to discover exactly what had occurred. A blue car had chased her, and she wondered about the driver. How far had he been prepared to go? Had his intention been merely to frighten her? Was she now expected to run to Wayne with a plea to him to buy the plantation?

The muted roaring of the waves hammering the reef lulled her and she was ready to sleep, despite the thoughts hammering inside her head. She turned away from the window, but at that moment there was a movement in the garden below.

She gazed into the darkness, thinking she was mistaken, then an indistinct figure moved out from the shadow of a tree and flitted silently towards the cliff top where the steps led down to the beach. For a moment Selina was transfixed. Was Paul making a last round of the place? She pulled on her dressing-gown and went down to confront Joanne.

'There's someone prowling around out in the garden,' she said. Joanne was startled, then shook her head.

'The shadows are deceptive, Selina. I've often thought I've seen someone but it's turned out to be something quite innocent.'

'I'm certain! A figure was moving quite furtively.'

'In that case, we'll check it out or you won't sleep tonight.' Joanne rose and went to a cupboard to take out a powerful torch.

'Do you want to come along or shall I go alone?'

'I wouldn't dream of letting you go alone,' Selina replied. 'Where's Paul?'

'He's gone to take a look along the road to the north to see if he can find out what happened to you.'

Joanne was looking pale, shocked almost as much as Selina herself.

'Perhaps it would be wiser to wait for him to come home.'

'We never have any trouble of that nature around here.'

'Then let's forget about it.'

Selina wasn't keen to go out into the darkness.

'Whoever it was went towards the steps leading down to the beach. I expect he's gone now.'

'You actually saw a figure? Are you sure?'

'It certainly wasn't my imagination,' Selina responded.

At that moment, the sound of an approaching car cut through the silence, and Joanne smiled.

'Here's Paul now! He'll look around.'

They went out to the veranda as Paul alighted from his car. Joanne handed him the torch. He looked startled for a moment, but as she explained, he hurried off to the cliff top. Selina remained on the veranda, Joanne with her.

'Are you of a nervous disposition?' Joanne queried. 'It is quite isolated out here. When Paul and I move back to our house you'd better have a houseboy as well as a cook and maid.'

'I'm not normally nervous, but after what's happened today I'd be a fool to take risks. I think someone is trying to frighten me into selling out.'

'Someone?' Joanne's face was shadowed. 'There's only one man around here who wants to buy this place, and that's Hank Wayne!'

'What about Zack?'

'Zack! He's the last man I'd suspect! He has the best interests of the plantation at heart. I'd never believe Zack would use such tactics to get you out.'

Selina didn't reply and they waited in silence, until Paul returned.

'I didn't see anyone or hear anything suspicious,' he reported. 'Could it have been your imagination, Selina?'

'I'm certain it wasn't,' she replied firmly. 'I saw a movement beside that tree over there, and saw a figure move out of the shadows and cross to the top of the cliff.'

'I'll take a look around in the morning when it's light,' Paul promised. 'There might be footprints. But I wouldn't worry too much about it. The house is always locked up securely.'

'I was telling Selina we've never had that kind of trouble around here,' Joanne said.

'So it started with my arrival!' Selina observed. 'Isn't that a good indication that I'm the target?'

'That's true, but we won't take any chances after this,' Paul replied.

Selina went back to her room and stood in the darkness peering intently at the garden, and now the shadows seemed to be playing tricks. She could imagine figures everywhere, and drew a deep breath as she fought to control her nerves. She finally convinced herself there was nothing suspicious and went to bed, to sleep soundly until morning.

The sun was peeping in at the window when Selina awoke. She lay motionless until her thoughts fell into place. She rose swiftly, crossing to the window to peer out at the day. Then she looked down at the tree where she had seen the figure the night before and frowned.

What was happening to her? Was someone deliberately trying to frighten her? She instinctively suspected Hank Wayne. But what of Zack? He had expressed a desire to buy the plantation. And then there was Fiona. The girl was besotted with Zack, and seemed wilfully over-emotional.

She was thoughtful as she showered, still shocked by what had occurred. Then she dressed and went down to sit on the veranda. Joanne seemed to be apprehensive as they ate breakfast, served by Alora.

They were sipping fresh orange juice when Zack arrived. He mounted the steps to the veranda, and Selina's pulses quickened at the sight of his lean body in a T-shirt and beige shorts. His tanned face was creased by a cheerful smile.

'Good morning,' he greeted lightly. 'How are you feeling now your first full day is behind you?'

'You obviously haven't heard what happened to Selina last night,' Joanne said before Selina could reply.

Zack frowned and looked questioningly at Selina, then listened silently as Joanne explained about the unknown blue car. His features hardened as the frightening experience was related.

'I can't believe this,' he said when Joanne finished. 'And I considered driving you home last night! If only I had!' He shook his head, frowning. 'It must have been a joy-rider! There's too much of that sort of thing going on these days. Have the police been in touch with you this morning?'

'Not yet,' Joanne said.

'Inspector Fallon is a friend of mine. I'll call him. May I use your phone?'

Selina nodded and he went inside. She could hear his voice as he made a call, and moments later he returned to the veranda, still frowning.

'I spoke to John. They found the blue car last night on the rocks at the foot of the cliff at Carr Point. It was deserted, and there was no sign of the driver. They think it was deliberately driven over the cliff. The car belongs to Frank Taylor, Colonel Stuart's estate manager. He had reported it stolen in St Honoria earlier last evening.'

'But was it a joy-rider?' Joanne's voice was tense. 'Twice yesterday Selina was involved in road incidents, and I think that's once too often to be mere coincidence!'

'So do I,' Selina retorted.

Zack shook his head, his expression grim.

'If that's true then this is serious,' he

observed. 'And if it was deliberate then we don't have far to look for the culprit.'

'Hank Wayne? Would he go that far to get this property?'

'I've heard some very nasty tales about his business methods,' Zack said reluctantly. 'But I can't believe he'd go that far.'

He accepted a coffee from the attentive Alora and sat down in the shade.

'There was someone prowling around the garden last night,' Selina said.

He gazed at her in disbelief.

'Are you sure?'

'Quite.'

She explained what had happened.

'I'll take a look around.'

'I'll show you where I first saw the figure, and where he walked. There may be footprints. Paul said he was going to check this morning, but I want to look for myself.'

'Can you be certain it was a man?' he asked as they went down into the garden.

Selina was startled, and he smiled and shrugged.

'It could have been Alora, making for a rendezvous with her boy-friend!'

'I'm sure it was a man,' she said firmly.

'Then it might have been Alora's boy-friend on his way home.'

Selina nodded, but wasn't convinced. Zack paused and looked back to see Alora emerging from the house to clear the breakfast table on the veranda.

'Did you see Charlie last night, Alora?' he asked.

'No, Mr Zack. He not come to see me last night. He go out fishing all night.'

'Did someone else come and see you in his place?'

'Mr Zack, you know I'm not a girl like that!'

Alora chuckled and went back into the house.

'Well, that lets Alora out,' he commented.

Selina looked around intently when

they reached the tree where she had seen the figure, but there was nothing to see. She led the way to the top of the cliff where she had seen the figure walking.

'I wouldn't attach too much importance to the incident,' Zack decided. 'Anyone going between the village and St Honoria would probably walk along the beach and use your steps here because it's a lot quicker than walking on the road from town.'

Selina nodded but wasn't convinced. Zack changed the subject.

'The simple way to guard against anything else happening is always to have someone with you,' he said. 'What do you plan to do today?'

'I'd like to look around the plantation.'

'Good. Would you like me to show you around?'

'Yes, please, if you're not busy.'

They returned to the veranda where Joanne greeted Selina with a smile.

'Fiona just telephoned,' Joanne said,

'She asked for you, Selina, but when I told her Zack was here she hung up.'

'I wonder what she wanted?' Selina recalled Fiona's attitude the previous evening, and the fact that the blue car chasing her last night belonged to Colonel Stuart's estate manager seemed to give substance to her suspicion that Fiona had given way to jealousy and tried to remove her.

'I expect she wants to make friends,' Zack said with a grin.

'If I know Fiona, she'd have an ulterior motive if she did try to make friends,' Joanne retorted.

'I'll call her,' Selina decided. 'If she wants to be friendly, then the least I can do is meet her halfway.'

'You'll find her number in the book beside the telephone,' Joanne said.

Selina turned to the house, then paused and looked at Zack.

'Did you see Fiona last night after we parted?' she asked.

He shook his head.

'I didn't go looking for her, if that's

what you mean.'

'That's not what I mean. Did you see her in town after we parted?'

'No. She wasn't in any of her usual haunts, which is unusual in itself because she's always at the centre of whatever is going on in St Honoria. But surely you don't suspect her of trying to run you off the road!'

'The car belonged to her father's estate manager,' Selina mused. 'It would have been easy for her to get hold of it.'

Zack's face was grim, but he did not scoff at her words.

'I wouldn't put it past her,' he said slowly. 'She is capable of anything, given the motive. But leave it to me. I can easily check on her movements last night. Call her and see why she rang you this morning. If she was driving that blue car last night then she'd want to know what state you're in this morning.'

Selina nodded and went into the house. She dialled Fiona's number, and

124

a moment later a female native voice answered. Asking for Fiona, Selina was told that she had left the house. Leaving a message that she had called, Selina returned to the veranda.

'She's out at the moment,' she said. 'Perhaps she'll contact me later.'

'I'll call John Fallon again and tell him of your suspicions,' Zack said. 'He'll make some enquiries, and I hope, for her sake, that Fiona knows nothing about that business last night.'

Selina shook her head, not knowing what to think. She was inclined to think it was all a bad dream. But she could hear Zack's voice as he spoke to Inspector Fallon, and his words rekindled the fear she had felt out there on the coast road. She sat down on the veranda and tried to relax but her heart was thudding and her palms were clammy.

'I'm going to look round the plantation today, Joanne,' she said, 'and Zack will accompany me.'

'You couldn't have a better guide than Zack.' Joanne smiled. 'Will you come back here for lunch?'

'No, thanks,' Zack replied from the doorway of the house. 'I plan to take Selina on to my place for lunch. I anticipated today's itinerary, and left instructions with my housekeeper to have lunch ready for us at one o'clock. But if Selina doesn't feel up to a full day out we can easily change our plans.'

'I feel quite all right!' Selina observed. 'In fact I'd rather get out and about and busy myself.'

'We ought to start now if you're to see everything,' Zack said.

They took their leave of Joanne, and as they went to his car, Zack glanced at Selina, his expression filled with concern.

'You're looking strained,' he observed. 'Are you sure you're up to a tour today?'

'Yes.' She nodded. 'I shall be all right.'

'The island seems to be agreeing with you.'

'So it should! I was born here. Are you native to the island? You seem to know all about me but I've learned nothing about your background.'

'I was born here, too,' he said as he started the car. They moved smoothly away from the veranda. 'My grandfather arrived from England in the Twenties and bought our place, and my father took over after the Second World War. I assumed control when Father died. That's why I'm so keen to preserve the island as it is. Generations of hard-working people have given their lives to provide the peace and tranquillity we have today, and I'll do whatever I can to perpetuate the standards we enjoy.'

Selina frowned, his words making her aware of the deeper issues behind Hank Wayne's desire to turn the island into a leisure centre. But that wouldn't happen because she had no intention of selling no matter what pressures were brought to bear on her. She looked at Zack, thankful that they were on the same side of the fence, and if he were telling the truth then there was no reason why he would want to harm her. The knowledge heartened her and she began to look forward to the day's outing.

When they reached the road, Zack turned away from St Honoria to ascend a steep hill surmounted by tall trees. Selina looked around with interest, and when the trees petered out and fields appeared in a vast patchwork below them, he pulled up on the verge and switched off.

'Let's get out for a moment,' he suggested.

Selina alighted and gazed around. On her left were fields and on the right was the coastline. She caught her breath at the view of Barracuda Bay from this height. Zack stood motionless at her side, and the intense silence around them was like a shield against reality.

'The island looks quite large,' she observed.

'It's about seventy miles long and half as wide,' he replied. 'There was quite a lot of volcanic action in this area millions of years ago.'

She nodded, turning her back on the coast to look at the extinct volcano towering over the centre of the island.

'Can you point out my boundaries from here?' she asked.

He raised an arm.

'The shore as far as you can see is yours, which is why Hank Wayne has been so anxious to do business with you.' He turned to his left, indicating the coast they had not yet visited. 'And you own all that up to and including the northern promontory, Carr Point, beyond which are cliffs with no beach.'

He turned his back to the coast.

'Inland, most of what you see is yours, and there is more behind that ridge running north to south. The buildings forming your plantation head-quarters are hidden in the valley beyond the ridge, and so is the village where your field hands live.'

Selina, aware that Zack was watching her, was suddenly afraid that she had too much to learn about this new way of life.

'We'll drive down to the village,' he said. 'With any luck we should see Paul at headquarters. This is his busy time right now but he's nearing the end of the spring planting.'

'And your place?' she enquired.

'I finished planting this week. That's why I'm able to relax a bit now.'

'So I've arrived at just the right time.'

'In more ways than one.'

He smiled.

Selina was thoughtful as they continued. When they crossed the ridge, she saw a village in the middle distance, with a cluster of barns and buildings to the left. Figures were moving in the fields.

Selina looked around with interest when they reached the collection of houses of all shapes and sizes that served the field workers. Chickens, sheep and goats were wandering around quite freely and there was a profusion of dogs, while some boys were playing cricket on an improvised pitch.

Zack didn't stop in the village but went on to headquarters, passing a big American car that was just leaving. The car's windows were tinted and Selina was unable to see the occupants.

'That's the car Hank Wayne is using on the island,' Zack said. 'What's he doing here?'

Selina gazed after the departing car, a shiver running through her when she pictured Wayne's harsh face and stony eyes. Zack parked in front of the office and Paul appeared, alerted by the sound of their arrival.

'Hello!' he greeted. 'I expect you're wanting to know what makes the plantation tick. We're nearly over our busy time, and then I'll be able to give you my full attention.'

'What was Hank Wayne doing here?' Selina demanded.

'Wayne?' Paul looked startled for a moment, then smiled. 'Oh, you mean the car that just left! Wayne has been using it. He hires it from Tom Parker. But he left the island last night and Tom brought his daughter to the office in it. She works here as my secretary.'

'Has Wayne gone for good?' Zack asked.

'Parker didn't say.'

Paul turned to Selina.

'How are you feeling after that business last night?'

'A bit shaken,' she admitted. 'But I won't take any chances after this.'

Paul looked over his shoulder when a voice called to him from the office.

'Excuse me!' he said apologetically. 'An important phone call.'

'We'll look around.' Selina smiled. 'See you later, Paul.'

He nodded and hurried back to his office. Selina looked at Zack.

'What now?' she queried.

'We'll go on to my place. You'll pick up all you need to know about the plantation as time goes by.'

He led her back to his car, his face intent, and she shivered as she leaned towards him, feeling his magnetism bridging the narrow distance between them.

She watched him as he drove along a narrow, uneven road that led inland. She suppressed a sigh, feeling as if she were sitting on a powder keg, disconcerted by the way her instincts were undermining her commonsense, and an underlying tension boded ill for her peace of mind.

Twice yesterday, she could easily have been killed, and if someone was that determined to get rid of her then she had to take the threat seriously.

6

Selina admired the scenery as Zack drove on. Mango trees were growing in profusion along the line of the road, the fields were green with growing cane, and here and there they passed clusters of small houses.

Estate workers were busy in the fields, planting sugar cane, each plant about two feet tall, and Selina could hear their voices raised in song. The miles of exotic scenery slipped by and, when they passed over a crest, she saw a bungalow in the distance, gleaming in the sunlight, with a terracotta tiled roof and cool, white walls.

'My place,' Zack said. 'It's not as large or as well situated as yours but it has been home to several generations of Hallidays.'

'It's beautiful!'

Selina gazed at the low building.

There was a long veranda running the length of the front which provided shade for the main rooms, and nearby trees afforded more shade.

Zack stopped the car in front of three wooden steps leading to a veranda, and as they alighted, a West Indian male emerged from the bungalow, grinning widely.

'It's all right, Charlie,' Zack said. 'Leave the car where it is.'

Charlie nodded and turned to disappear into the bungalow again but Zack called to him and he turned, smiling and nodding.

'This is Charlie, Alora's boy-friend,' Zack explained to Selina. 'Charlie, did you visit Alora at the Carr house last night?'

'No, sir. I fishing.'

Charlie gazed at Selina, who could tell by his physique that it was not his figure she had seen in her garden.

Zack led Selina on to the veranda and seated her in a cane chair before leaving her to go indoors. Selina relaxed, thankful for the shade. Her mind was teeming with the impressions she had gained during the morning, and excitement bubbled beneath the surface of her mind as the shock of the incidents of yesterday faded.

A car suddenly appeared on the road, and Selina frowned as it raised dust in its race towards the bungalow. It was a red, low, sleek sports model, approaching very fast. As it drew nearer, Selina saw a blonde head behind the wheel — Fiona!

The car looked as if it would crash headlong into the veranda, but brakes squealed and it halted inches from the wooden steps. Selina shook her head, vowing never to accept a lift from the girl, and noted Fiona's grim expression as she sprang out of the car and came bounding up the steps.

'Where's Zack?' she demanded curtly.

'Inside. How are you today, Fiona?'

'Not very pleased!'

'You telephoned me this morning,' Selina said as the girl turned to the door of the house.

'Yes.' Fiona paused. 'I was going to arrange to call on you. But I'll be busy all today so I'll ring you again when I'm free.'

'Fine.'

Selina wondered why Fiona would want to visit her when she could barely conceal her hostility, and watched silently as Fiona strode to the door, her shoulders held stiffly. She disappeared into the bungalow, but backed out again immediately as Zack emerged, carrying a tray of cold drinks.

'I heard you arrive!' he greeted. 'You'll come to grief one day, driving like that.' He paused. 'I told you I'd be busy all today, so what are you doing here?'

'Father wants to see you urgently, and I decided to deliver the message personally.'

'It would have been less wearing all round if he had telephoned,' Zack observed drily.

'He did, and was told you would not

be back until about this time.' Fiona glared at him. 'You should consider the consequences before making him take a back seat.'

'Sit down and have a drink before you leave.'

Zack calmly ignored her threat.

'You're looking quite overheated,' he added cheekily.

'No thanks to the offer of a drink. I have to get back. We're entertaining business people from the States and Father thinks you should meet them.'

Selina experienced a pang at the girl's words, aware that Zack's business with Fiona's father had to do with buying her estate. But Zack shook his head.

'I can't come now. We're about to have lunch. Anyway, I had a word with your father last evening. Perhaps you'll tell him I won't be free until later today. I'll call and see him then.'

'This business is important!' Fiona turned away. 'I'll tell Father what you said, and inform him of your attitude. If you want his help, Zack, then you'd better get your priorities right.'

'Just a moment.' Zack's voice was suddenly much harsher. 'Where were you last evening, Fiona?'

'What business is it of yours?' she countered, tossing her head.

'When there's trouble on the island, you're never far from its source,' he replied.

'I know what you're talking about, and Inspector Fallon called me, if you must know, and asked what my movements were last evening. I told him, because it is his business, but it's not yours, so if you want to know you'll have to ask the Inspector.'

Fiona ran down the veranda steps and jumped into her car. She engaged the gears harshly, whirled the vehicle around, and set off at a terrific pace, raising dust along the whole stretch of road.

Selina watched disapprovingly until the vehicle disappeared, wondering if Fiona had been driving that blue car the previous evening.

'She could give perfect lessons on how not to drive a car,' Zack observed.

'Shouldn't you go and see her father?' Selina countered. 'If it's business then you should attend to it. I wouldn't let the grass grow under my feet!'

'The situation has changed since I first approached the Colonel, as I explained to him last evening.'

'You mean you're certain now that I won't sell the plantation!' Selina nodded. 'But the Colonel thinks you should meet his new contacts in case the situation reverts.'

Zack put the tray on the table, and poured her a glass of orange juice. Selina sipped it, appreciating the sharp citrus sweetness as it moistened her parched throat. But she was perturbed by Fiona's attitude. The girl was unfriendly, jealous because of Zack's attention to his new neighbour, and she studied him, wondering about his relationship with Fiona.

'I'll show you around the place shortly,' he said, pouring himself a drink before sitting down. 'But first things first.'

He smiled, and she watched him, noting every nuance of expression flitting across his face.

'You're thoughtful,' he observed at length.

'I have a great deal to consider, what with this trouble I've had on the road. Do you think those incidents were mere coincidence or is someone trying to frighten me?'

He shook his head, his expression grave.

'I don't know what to think, but we won't take any chances. From now on, I'm going to be a second shadow to you, and if anyone is trying to scare you off the island then I'll be in a position to stop him.'

He leaned forward, smiling, to take the sting out of his words.

'Would you like more orange?'

'No, thank you.'

'Then may I show you around my humble abode?'

He stood up and held open the door for her. As soon as she stepped inside the front door of the bungalow, Selina was enamoured by the place. Honey-coloured stone tiles covered the entrance hall, with long raffia mats adding a homely touch.

A number of varnished doors led off the hall. Zack took her on a tour which revealed four bedrooms, a sitting-room and a dining-room with french windows opening on to a patio leading to a large, rectangular swimming pool.

Maria, Zack's housekeeper, announced that lunch was ready, and proceeded to serve them on the veranda. Selina enjoyed the cold salad, and Zack relaxed as they ate, talking of sugar cane and what the business could expect in the year ahead.

'You've become quite thoughtful,' he observed, when the meal was over. 'Has Fiona's attitude upset you?'

'I'm more concerned that I might be taking up too much of your time,' she replied. 'While it's admirable to help out a new neighbour, there has to be a limit. But apart from that, I have no wish to make enemies of anyone on the island.'

He smiled, but his expression hardened momentarily.

'Hank Wayne is the only one here who would give you trouble.'

He pushed back his chair and stood up.

'It looks as if you've finished. Out here one usually rests after a meal, but we can move on if you like.'

'What about Hank Wayne?' she demanded. 'How far do you think he would go to get my plantation? He seemed very intense to me. I found him quite intimidating. He said he's spent a great deal of money on a feasibility study.'

'He's certainly spent a great deal of time and money on the project, and then you turned up flatly refusing to sell.'

'Are you saying that he can't take no for an answer?'

'I think he is finding it difficult to accept your attitude, and may use high-pressured business methods to persuade you to change your mind.'

'Such as frightening me into selling? He'll waste more time and money if he is trying that because I have no intention of selling, and I won't be intimidated!' She sighed. 'Perhaps I should go home now,' she suggested. 'Joanne and Paul are thinking of moving back to their home now I'm settling in. I ought to see if there is anything I can do to help them.'

'Joanne will arrange a cook, a maid and a houseboy for you, and they will take care of everything. For this afternoon I suggest a trip to the interior. I expect you'd like to freshen up before facing the sun again.'

'Thank you, I would!'

Selina rose, aware that Fiona's intrusion and hostile attitude had taken the shine off her pleasure, and she was perturbed by Zack's inference that Hank Wayne might not accept her decision not to sell . . .

They spent the afternoon sight-seeing, and by the time Zack called a halt, Selina was exhausted.

'I really must go home, shower and change my clothes,' she said.

'Fine.'

He turned the car and drove along the coast road.

'I have to see the Colonel and catch up on business. I'll pick you up later.'

She nodded and he drove her home.

'See you in about three hours,' he suggested.

'Thank you.'

Selina closed the car door and he departed. She gazed after him, then turned thoughtfully and entered the house.

'Had a nice day?' Joanne enquired.

'Yes, thanks. But right now I can't think beyond a cold shower and a change of clothes.'

'I know exactly how you feel!' Joanne laughed. 'You look as if you've had your fair share of the sun today. Are you hungry?'

'No thanks! I lunched at Zack's place.'

'By the way, I'm moving back to my place tomorrow, Selina. I've arranged for a housekeeper to call early in the morning to meet you. Alora will stay on as your maid.'

'Fine. But, Joanne, you don't have to consider moving until you're quite ready. I enjoy your company.'

'It's more convenient for Paul to be at our place. He'll be nearer the job, for one thing. And you need your privacy. But don't think I'm deserting you. If anything crops up you have only to telephone.'

'Thank you.' Selina smiled. 'I'll take a shower now and rest for a bit. I'm exhausted.'

She went up to her room and undressed, then stepped thankfully under the shower, sighing in relief as the cool water struck her skin. She remained under the stream of water until her body temperature returned to normal, then dried herself and donned a cotton dress before stretching out on the bed. Stifling a yawn, she closed her eyes and relaxed, succumbing to blissful sleep.

Later, she awoke and lay gazing around while her mind struggled back to the present. Raising herself up on one elbow, she peered through the window and saw the waves at their eternal task of hammering the distant reef. So it was not all a marvellous dream. She really was on Tarango and Zack was solid reality.

She slid off the bed and stood up, feeling completely refreshed. Looking at her watch, she was surprised to find that she had slept for two hours. It was time to start thinking of dressing for the evening.

She was undecided what to wear, but chose a pale blue dress with a flared skirt and full sleeves. She attended to her make-up with meticulous care, then went down to the veranda, where Alora told her that Joanne had gone into town.

The sound of an approaching car could be heard and Selina's pulses raced as she anticipated Zack's arrival. But it was Paul, and he looked tired when he stepped on to the veranda.

'Had a good day?' he enquired.

'I have indeed. But you look exhausted!'

He smiled.

'It's the heat more than the amount of work. But we are well ahead with the planting and everything is running sweetly. I'm sorry I hadn't time to show you around earlier but when the planting is finished things will be much easier, and then we can get together and I'll explain the business.'

'Fine, but there's no urgency. I'm merely curious about the way things work around here.'

Selina heard another car approaching and glanced beyond Paul's sturdy figure to see Zack's car arriving. He came on to the veranda, and Selina studied him while he chatted with Paul. He had changed his clothes, she noticed.

'You're looking very much refreshed,' he observed when Paul withdrew into the house.

He sat down opposite Selina and reached across the table to grasp her hand in a friendly gesture.

'Are you ready for this evening?'

'That depends on what you have planned,' she replied. 'It will have to be restful. I'm feeling just a little bit fragile.'

'We'll spend the time out of the sun.'

He smiled, and Selina realised that his mannerisms were becoming familiar to her.

'Would you like some tea?' she enquired.

'No, thanks.'

He glanced at his watch.

'We'd better leave. I've reserved a table at a restaurant, and I don't want to hurry you.'

Selina rose and he escorted her to his car. Excitement began to weave its spell upon her and she revelled in the exotic atmosphere. They drove into St Honoria and parked close to the yacht marina. The evening was perfect, the view to the horizon across the tangle of yacht masts stimulating her imagination.

Calypso music was being played softly in the background and a cooling breeze was rustling through the swaying coconut palms. Zack conducted her to the veranda of a restaurant overlooking the harbour and an attentive waiter showed them to a table which had an uninterrupted view of the bay. She looked at Zack to find he was watching her, and he smiled as their glances met.

'What would you like to drink?' he asked.

'Anything you suggest,' she replied.

He called a waiter, and moments later she was sipping an amber-coloured drink with ice and fruit on top, which proved to be refreshingly delicious. Zack checked the menu, and she studied him in detail while he was occupied.

'Perhaps you'd better approach our more exotic dishes with some caution,' he observed, looking over the menu at her.

She selected shrimp with deep-fried vegetable while he ordered fillet steak. The meal was perfect, the white Californian wine Zack ordered suiting the palate. Selina discovered that she was hungry, and Zack attacked his steak with gusto.

She was thrilled by her exotic surroundings, her attention drawn to his impressive figure across the table. They had spent many hours together since her arrival and she was now feeling at ease in his company. They were strangers no longer.

After the meal, they adjourned to the veranda overlooking the bay and sat in comfortable easy chairs in the shade. Selina marvelled at the view and relaxed despite the fear still bubbling in the back of her mind.

Presently, the waiter came to Zack's side and bent to whisper in his ear. Zack frowned and got to his feet, his face serious as he looked at Selina.

'Excuse me,' he said. 'Fiona is making a fool of herself in the bar and I'd better intervene. I'll be back shortly.'

Selina frowned as he departed, picturing Fiona's wilful face. The girl obviously had no intention of losing Zack without a fight. She shook her head, unaware of the situation that had existed before her arrival. Minutes passed before Zack reappeared and sat down beside her.

'I'm sorry,' he said. 'I've managed to get Fiona into the manager's office but I'm going to have to take her home. I'll be about thirty minutes. Will you wait here for me?'

'I wouldn't dare go home alone,' Selina said instantly.

'You'll be quite safe here. I'd take you along in the car but Fiona is spoiling for a fight and she'd probably create a scene if she saw you. Have another drink and enjoy the view. I won't be long.'

'Fine.'

Selina fought down her disappointment, and sighed as Zack departed.

The evening was still young, the sun dappling the calm water of the bay. Selina looked over at the yacht marina and saw *Trade Wind* at her mooring. On an impulse she arose and walked to the edge of the veranda, feeling an urge to visit the boat and perhaps chat with Bill Sharpley. The waiter approached and Selina turned to him.

'When Mr Halliday returns, please tell him I've gone to see Bill Sharpley.'

'Mr Halliday told me to keep an eye on you while he was away,' the waiter admitted. 'Don't you think you'd better wait here until he returns?'

'It's such a lovely evening, and he'll be back before dark,' she said.

The waiter nodded and moved away, and Selina left the restaurant to walk along the jetty to Bill Sharpley's place.

She reached his office, and was surprised to find it deserted and locked for Bill haunted this place day and night. Then she saw a notice in a window stating that he was delivering a boat to a customer along the coast and wouldn't be back until midnight.

She walked along the jetty to *Trade Wind*, pausing now and again to look back for signs of Zack. She reached the boat and stepped aboard to stand at the wheel, gripping it as thoughts of her father filtered into her mind. None of this uncertainty would have occurred if he had been alive, she thought.

She let herself into the cabin area but the air was stale and she returned to the cockpit to breathe deeply of the sweet evening air, her nerves badly over-stretched. She had an impulse to sail the boat around the bay. She had watched Zack's routine for handling the craft, and knew she had to start learning to stand on her own two feet. She turned her attention to the controls.

Turning on the fuel switch, she ensured the gear lever was in neutral before pressing the starter button. The powerful engine roared and she drew a deep breath, gripped by sudden excitement. She needed to do some things on her own, and right now she had an urge to handle the boat.

She returned to the jetty to untie the mooring lines, cast off, and went back aboard, slipping the engine into gear and opening the throttle. The boat moved ahead and she turned the wheel slightly, curving away from the jetty.

Exhilaration gripped her as she set course for the far side of the bay, keeping a sharp lookout as she did so. The radio was close at hand and she switched it on to listen to the chatter on the air. The switches on the radio were clearly marked and she familiarised herself with them until she was certain she knew what to do.

Soon she was handling the boat as if she had been doing it all her life, and enjoyed the peacefulness and solitude of the evening. She changed course and began to angle towards the reef, but stayed well away from the tide race coming through the gap. The sight of the crashing rollers was awesome, and she listened to the dull pounding of the breakers and saw spray flying.

From this point, it seemed impossible that anyone could take a vessel through that area, and yet she knew that with practice she would be able to do so without hesitation. But at the moment she wished the reef was non-existent because she could not reach the open sea.

Looking around, she spotted a large cabin cruiser coming up from behind, obviously heading for the gap, and wondered who was aboard. She watched with interest as the craft approached, then realised it seemed to be coming too close to her.

She stiffened with horror as its sharp bow missed her stern by only a few feet. In passing, it was so close it almost scraped the paint off the side of *Trade Wind*.

There were two men in the cockpit, one steering and the other sitting in the stern, and when the cockpits of the two vessels were level and only a foot or so apart, the sitting man sprang up and jumped across the space between the vessels to land rather clumsily right alongside Selina!

Before she could grasp what was happening, he thrust her aside and took hold of the wheel. Opening the throttle, he sent *Trade Wind* forward, falling in behind the larger craft which was heading towards the gap in the reef.

It was then Selina recognised the man who had come aboard, and a spasm of fear caused her breath to catch in her throat. It was Pete Brewer, Hank Wayne's man! He turned a grim face towards her.

'You'd better sit down and hang on,' he rasped. 'We're going out through the gap.'

'What are you doing?' she gasped.

'Turn the boat and take me back to the shore!'

Brewer laughed, ignoring her demand, and turned his attention to the reef. Selina clasped her hands together, unable to believe what was happening. The next instant *Trade Wind* was caught up in the disturbed water of the gap, and she was terrified by the sight of the raging maelstrom ahead.

They began to dip and roll, surging forward to the point of no return, and were encompassed by the spray that hung like a glittering curtain over the gap. She clung to a stanchion, dazed by the turn of events, and cold fear filled her when she realised that she was being kidnapped!

Now she knew for certain who was behind her troubles, and it was too late for her to do anything about it.

7

Selina was so shocked she could only sit helplessly in the stern of *Trade Wind*, grasping the stanchion as Pete Brewer negotiated the gap. He was not as skilful as Zack, and took the boat through the reef in a series of violent manoeuvres before gaining the calmer sea beyond.

The yacht which had brought Brewer out to *Trade Wind* was standing by, clear of the reef, and Brewer steered towards it until he was close enough to communicate.

'I'll sail out to sea and make it back just after dark,' he shouted. 'Be here waiting for me, Al.'

The man in the other boat nodded and waved, and Brewer turned to Selina.

'Go into the cabin and stay there,' he ordered.

'You'd better take me back to the shore,' she said tremulously.

'We'll be coming back later.'

He grasped her arm and conducted her to the cabin area, pushing her into the large cabin.

'Just stay quiet,' he snapped.

When he departed, Selina locked the door on the inside and sank down on a bunk. Her thoughts were beginning to tick over again and she dearly wished she had listened to Zack and stayed at the restaurant until he returned. But what did Hank Wayne hope to gain by having her kidnapped? Surely he knew he could not scare her into selling the plantation.

The answer that came to her was so frightening she tried not to consider it, but was forced to think it through. Brewer said he was coming back to the gap after dark, which could only mean that he did not want to risk being seen in his plan to set her adrift so that she died in the fury of crashing white water. If she were dead Hank Wayne might get his hands on the estate, and he knew it was the only chance he had.

But she couldn't believe anyone would go to such lengths to clinch a deal. Yet, picturing Wayne's face, she suppressed a shiver, quite able to believe him capable of anything.

Facing the grim knowledge of what was likely to happen, Selina discovered a reserve of determination she hadn't known she possessed, and became less afraid. Determination gripped her, for she was aware that she could either sit waiting for the inevitable to happen or make a desperate effort to escape the grim situation that had enveloped her. But what could she do?

She looked around the cabin, hoping to find something she could use as a weapon. Brewer was a powerful man, but if she took him by surprise she just might get the better of him. And she knew she would have only one chance. If she failed in her first attempt, she would be completely at his mercy.

But the cabin was bare. Even the

bunks were not made up. She was gripped by despair until her searching gaze spotted a hatch set in the deck above, close to the bows, which gave access to the tiny foredeck overhead and served as a means of escape in case of emergency.

Two large bolts on the inside secured the hatch, and Selina tried them, finding, to her surprise, that they moved easily. She paused, frantically wondering what she could do. Glancing through the porthole, she saw that night was closing in. Darkness would fall in about thirty minutes, so Brewer would be turning back to the gap at any time.

She decided to wait until darkness came before attempting anything, and the minutes dragged by as she forced herself to remain motionless on the bunk. But fear ate into her determination. Her mind was still partially blanketed by shock, and as time passed her nerves began to suffer from the growing tension.

She looked at her hands, saw they

were trembling, and clenched them. She had to remain strong, aware that if she gave way to her fears, she would make Brewer's job that much easier. She got up and began to pace the cabin, trying to keep her thoughts off what might be about to happen.

Daylight was fading outside the porthole when Selina felt the boat keel over as it turned to make the return trip to the gap. She staggered sideways as the deck tilted, throwing out her arms to maintain her balance. Her right hand struck the handle of a small cabinet.

She instinctively gripped it to save her balance and the handle moved, her weight dragging the door open. Selina fell against the bulkhead and slid to the floor. The boat straightened up again and she dragged herself upright. When she glanced into the cabinet, her pulses raced at the sight of a flare pistol and a box of distress flares nestling inside.

She checked that the cabin door was locked then picked up the gun and examined it meticulously, discovering how it worked. She loaded it, took the box of flares, and went to the escape hatch, sliding out the bolts. By standing on a bunk and using her head and shoulders she managed to ease the hatch open, then she stood on the bunk with her head through the hatch, and looked into the shadows that had closed in.

She eased herself into a sitting position on the edge of the hatch with her back to the bows, estimating that they were about fifteen minutes from the reef. She was facing the cockpit, and could see the head and shoulders of Pete Brewer illuminated by the greenish light from the control panel.

Raising the flare pistol, she drew a deep breath to steady herself and fired it with the muzzle angled skywards. She flinched at the loud report, and quickly reloaded as the flare burst high overhead. Strangely, she was calm now, her actions under control, and when Brewer climbed towards her out of the cockpit, she pointed the flare pistol at him from the distance of only a few feet.

'If you come any closer I'll fire at you!' she called, her heart pounding furiously.

'Don't be a fool!' he replied. 'Put that down.'

He continued to ease out of the cockpit and Selina canted the muzzle of the pistol before firing. The flare sped in a fiery arc, closely passing by Brewer's head before striking the sea beyond the boat and spluttering upwards at an angle. Brewer tumbled back into the cockpit as Selina feverishly reloaded.

Her thoughts were fast-moving but calm, and realising that he might try to break down the cabin door and attack her from below, she slid on to the narrow foredeck, closed the hatch and bolted it on the outside. Then she crouched in the bows and awaited Brewer's reaction.

He kept below the level of the cockpit, and Selina was cheered by the fact that she had triumphed over him.

But it was stalemate. He couldn't get at her but she was trapped on the boat, and if he managed to get off at the gap then he could still achieve his object — setting her adrift alone in the wild sea, which would mean her certain death.

Minutes passed, and soon she heard the distant roar of waves crashing on the reef. She glanced around but could see nothing, for night had now closed in completely. She fired another flare, hoping that someone ashore would see it and raise the alarm. But she knew with a pang of despair that any boat putting out from the bay would arrive too late to help her. She had to take over control of *Trade Wind* if she was to have any chance of survival.

When she spotted the indistinct lights of another boat nearby, her heart leaped in relief, until she remembered the boat that had brought Brewer alongside. Her tension increased. Brewer's accomplice was waiting at the rendezvous as instructed.

The ceaseless roaring of the waves was filling the air with sullen noise, and Selina felt as if she were in the grip of a nightmare that would not go away. But she knew what she had to do. She must prevent the other boat from taking Brewer off *Trade Wind* so they could not abandon her to the reef.

Brewer spotted the other boat and turned towards it. Selina could see the pale face of the man in the other cockpit as the two craft converged. She pointed the gun in his direction and fired. The flare streaked low over the space between the two vessels and hit the side of the open cockpit. The craft immediately veered away.

'Brewer, keep away from that boat!' Selina shouted, twisting to keep the other craft in view as it began to circle them.

She watched its progress while keeping an eye on Brewer's position, afraid that he might be desperate enough to attempt to overpower her despite the threat of the flare pistol.

They were moving closer to the gap, and soon Selina could feel the pull of the waves that were surging and funnelling towards the reef.

* * *

They were still outside the main tidal race, but each moment was taking them closer. She wondered what Brewer would do. He had to leave the boat at the last moment, when it would be impossible for her to regain control and avoid the gap in the reef. She strained her eyes but could see no sign of him.

She was cowed by the menace of the pistol in her hands, and she was gripped by an unholy joy at the knowledge that she was equal to the needs of this fearful situation.

'Al,' Brewer called suddenly. 'Stand by to pick me up. I'll swim to you at the last moment.'

'I'm ready, Pete,' came the gruff reply.

Selina aimed at the cockpit of the

other boat and fired. The flare struck into it, almost hitting the man, and when it burst, she was shocked by the blaze that erupted. Flames shot upwards and she saw the man duck quickly out of sight.

Brewer's head and shoulders appeared at the stern and Selina fired in his general direction. He ducked immediately and she became aware that she had gained the initiative. But the boat was veering towards the other craft, and moments later Brewer dived over the side of *Trade Wind* and began to swim powerfully towards the other craft, where the man was using a fire extinguisher.

Selina watched intently, and within a few moments Brewer was clambering into the smouldering craft. He rushed to the wheel, spun it, and rapidly put distance between the two boats.

'It's all yours, lady!' he yelled at Selina.

She snapped out of the numbness gripping her, and, scrambling towards the cockpit, she took the flare gun and flares with her and dropped into the cockpit. She grabbed the wheel, watching the other boat, fearing a trick. But Brewer was dropping astern and turning away.

Selina offered up a silent prayer as she throttled up to full power and spun the wheel to veer away from the gap, aware that she could not negotiate it successfully. But if she could get well clear of the current she could await rescue. At that moment, the engine faltered in its steady rhythm, spluttering a number of times before resuming its steady throbbing.

Selina gasped, then sighed with relief as it picked up, but then the engine cut out completely and a frightening silence followed.

For a shocked moment she stood frozen in horror. The boat immediately began to rock slightly. Panic filled her as she put the gear lever into neutral and pressed the starter button. Nothing happened except a thin whirring sound as the boat began to drift stern-first towards the gap.

Frantically, she redoubled her efforts to restart the engine. But nothing she did had any effect and she turned her attention to the radio, movements feverish as she switched the instrument to transmit. Then she realised that the radio was dead! When she looked at the switches, she was horrified to see that the green light was out. She switched off and on several times without result. The radio was dead!

Trade Wind was drifting stern first towards the reef, and fear gripped Selina as she realised the helplessness of her situation. Evidently Brewer had done something to the engine before jumping overboard. She looked round and saw the other boat standing off at a distance. They were calmly watching her frantic struggle for survival.

Again she attempted to restart the engine but all she heard was a gurgle. The boat began to move faster as it was seized by the fearsome race of waves speeding towards the reef. She realised that the current was getting stronger, the waves rearing higher under the influence of the narrow gap. The sound of the breakers had increased and she shuddered as she felt the boat responding to the rising swell. Fear gripped her.

She tried the radio again, wondering why the green **ON** light had failed. Didn't that mean there was no power at all? She flicked the switches, thinking that she had inadvertently turned off the set, but nothing happened, the baffling silence prevailing.

The boat was now rocking more than ever. She glanced over the stern at the reef and was shocked by how near it seemed. Within a few minutes *Trade Wind* would be irretrievably caught and battered, then sucked under by the terrible fury of the sea.

She spun the steering-wheel without effect, and realised that without power the craft was helpless in the grip of the turbulent current. Then she was aware of a different sound and tried to pinpoint it, peering around desperately, but the flying spray over the gap blurred her vision and as the terrifying moments passed, she could only stand at the wheel, gripping it helplessly to maintain her balance and trying to reconcile herself to the fate that would inevitably over-whelm her.

A faint shadow moved in the very core of the white fury boiling in the gap, and Selina narrowed her eyes to pick out details. A boat was emerging from the very heart of the battering waves, and her heart leaped as it hurled itself towards her. It looked like Fiona's speedboat, and Selina was almost faint with relief.

Watching the craft intently, she saw two figures crouched in it as it came through the mass of waves like an arrow. She fired a flare skywards, although she did not doubt that she had been seen.

The speedboat cleared the gap and came curving towards her, white water spraying from its sharp bow. It swung in an arc, rapidly cutting down its speed, the roar of its engine diminishing, and finally it came alongside. A figure sprang from it, vaulting into the cockpit of *Trade Wind*, and Selina gasped when she recognised Zack.

Almost swooning in relief, she was aware of the speedboat swinging away and begin to circle just clear of the reef.

Zack barely glanced at Selina. He lunged to the controls and tried the engine, without result. Then he peered over the stern at the reef, which was frighteningly near.

'The radio is dead, too!' Selina called. 'There's no power!'

Zack nodded and reached to the side of the console, pulling open a hinged flap. For a tense moment he did something inside, his shadowed features intent, and Selina, watching closely, suddenly saw the green light on the engine control panel come on.

Zack closed the flap and pressed the starter button. The engine immediately fired and roared into life with full power, and Selina almost lost her balance as Zack thrust the engine into gear and spun the wheel to bring the bows around to face the gap. They were now too close to the reef to pull away.

'Brace yourself and hang on!' Zack yelled. 'We have to go through.'

Selina nodded and lunged towards the stern seat, grasping the stanchion as the boat rolled and dipped, now completely in the grip of the furious race of water surging into the narrow gap in the reef. She watched wide-eyed as Zack increased power and steered into the very heart of the surging foam.

She felt immense relief at his presence. He had come for her, and his arrival had left no leeway for safety. A few moments more and she would have been at the helpless mercy of this fury.

Zack fought the enormous force of the sea, spinning the wheel first one way and then the other, gauging their progress as he pitted his wits and reflexes against the awesome might of the elements. The engine was throbbing powerfully, and Selina held her breath as they dipped and lunged to left and right, carried remorselessly into the gap.

They had enough power to control their progress sufficiently to prevent the sea from overwhelming them. The roar of the waves battered her ears, and yet there was a fierce joy in her because Zack was in control and would save her from the ghastly death that had been planned for her.

After what seemed an eternity, they plunged through the gap and were swept into the calmer water of the bay. The frantic movements of the boat faded as they slid forward on an even keel, making for their distant mooring at the jetty.

★ ★ ★

Selina arose from her seat and lurched towards Zack, who throttled down the engine and turned to her. She reached out and grasped his shoulder and he slid a comforting arm around her slender shoulders.

'I couldn't believe it when I saw you drifting out here,' he said huskily.

'How did you know where to find me?' she demanded.

Her senses were in a whirl and she could feel reaction taking its toll of her overstretched nerves. She fought against an impulse to cry.

'I was taking Fiona home when I realised she had sobered up rather quickly since I saw her in the manager's office. Knowing her, I suspected she was up to no good, and had to get quite tough with her before she told me Brewer had arranged for her to get me away from you because it had been planned to put you in a car and drive you over a cliff!'

Selina gasped as the import of his words struck her, unable to believe that Fiona had succumbed so completely to her jealousy. Zack nodded grimly, his expression harsh in the greenish light reflecting from the controls.

'I warned you about Wayne,' he said,

'but even I didn't think he would go so far to gain control of your plantation. I thought Fiona was joking, but I rushed back to the restaurant in a panic. When the waiter told me you had gone to your boat, I feared the worst, especially when I got to the jetty and found *Trade Wind* gone from her moorings. And Bill Sharpley was nowhere around!

'I made Fiona take me out in her speedboat. I knew you had to be in the bay somewhere because you can't negotiate the gap in the reef. I didn't think for a moment that Brewer had got to you, and I was searching for *Trade Wind* when flares started exploding out beyond the reef. I couldn't believe it was you but I had to take a chance, so we came through the reef and there you were!'

Selina trembled as she explained what had happened, and tears of relief streamed down her cheeks. Zack embraced her consolingly, and she clung to him, seeking comfort. Reaction had set in and she shivered.

'What about Brewer and his accomplice?' she asked. 'They were watching me drifting into the gap.'

'They won't get away.'

Zack spoke grimly. He turned to the radio and began calling the local coastguard while Selina clung to him, unable to believe the danger was really over.

'I was doing all right until everything cut out!' she said when Zack turned to her again.

'You certainly did!' he said and reached for her again, and it was the most natural thing in the world for Selina to slip into his embrace.

'It's a pity Brewer removed a fuse from the back of the control panel before he left you. Until then you beat him at every turn. I'm proud of you.'

Then his voice turned brittle.

'It's a pity you didn't sink his boat. But the coastguards will soon pick him up, and when we get ashore, I'll inform the police about this and they'll pick up Hank Wayne. He's overstepped the mark this time, and there is proof against him.'

He smiled and drew her close, and Selina slid her arms around him and pressed her face into his comforting shoulder.

'I'll give you lessons on every aspect of sailing before you venture out here again,' he said softly. 'And I don't want to let you out of my sight ever again, Selina!'

He placed his hands against her face and tilted her head until she was looking up at him. Selina was very conscious of his nearness. She was still trembling because of the fright she had received, but from the moment Zack had climbed aboard she had felt safe.

'I shouldn't have trusted Fiona,' he said. 'And I never should have left you. Thank goodness I suspected her motives in time! A few minutes later and the worst could have happened.'

'I'd have tried to steer the boat through the gap without power,' Selina said tremulously.

'I haven't tried that myself yet,' he admitted, 'but if anyone could do it you could, I'm sure. You proved yourself to be more than a match for Hank Wayne.'

Selina caught her breath.

'He has to be at the back of all this,' she said softly.

'Even though he left the island the night before!' Zack nodded. 'I was hard on Fiona on our way out here, and she broke down and told me what was going on. Her jealousy goaded her into agreeing to help Wayne get you off the island.

'She said she didn't think he wanted anything more than that, but it was her idea to steal the car of her father's estate manager and try to run you off the road last night. She said she wasn't trying to kill you. She merely wanted to frighten you into leaving the island.'

'I saw her sitting with Wayne after she left us!' Selina suppressed a shiver. 'What will happen now, Zack?'

'This is so serious we must tell the police everything and let them sort it out,' he replied. 'Fiona has already agreed to go back to Europe and stay away. But enough of that. You've had more than enough for one day. I'll take you home.'

His arms tightened around her and Selina looked into his face as his lips came towards hers. She closed her eyes, and as his lips touched hers, the din of the waves seemed to fade.

She responded with growing passion. This was a man in a million, she thought, and now she was in his arms, the future seemed assured.

THE END

We do hope that you have enjoyed reading this large print book.

Did you know that all of our titles are available for purchase?

We publish a wide range of high quality large print books including:
Romances, Mysteries, Classics
General Fiction
Non Fiction and Westerns

Special interest titles available in large print are:
The Little Oxford Dictionary
Music Book, Song Book
Hymn Book, Service Book

Also available from us courtesy of Oxford University Press:
Young Readers' Dictionary
(large print edition)
Young Readers' Thesaurus
(large print edition)

For further information or a free brochure, please contact us at:
Ulverscroft Large Print Books Ltd.,
The Green, Bradgate Road, Anstey,
Leicester, LE7 7FU, England.
Tel: (00 44) 0116 236 4325
Fax: (00 44) 0116 234 0205

Other titles in the
Linford Romance Library:

A TIME FOR DREAMS

Dawn Bridge

Claire is a teacher awaiting an Ofsted inspection at her school. She discovers that the chief inspector is her former fiancé Adam whom she has not seen for five years. Although Claire is now in a relationship with Martin, she is overcome with guilt when she realises she still has feelings for Adam. Suddenly she has to confront her past and decisions have to be made.

THE HEART SHALL CHOOSE

Wendy Kremer

Roark is charming, but emotionally damaged by his broken marriage. Julia quit a relationship when she found her ex-boyfriend was exploiting her. Whilst Julia still hopes to find real love one day, Roark intends to shut love out of his life altogether. Working in a tour company together, their friendship grows — but can Julia storm the barriers that surround his heart? And can Roark forget the past and move on to a better future, before it's too late.

THE JUBILEE LETTER

Carol MacLean

The letter had been lost in the post for fifty years. But for Avril it solved a mystery, which had unsettled her since the Queen's Coronation — when she was young and in love . . . There had been two suitors to choose from: was Avril tempted by charming Jack or quiet Gordon? Both Jack and Gordon had secrets, and it was only when Avril discovered what they were hiding that she had been able to choose a love to last a lifetime.